Death and Games in Los Angeles . . .

Elysian Fields borders a golf course, and the hole they'd dug for Roger Scott was only about twenty yards from the fence that ran along the thirteenth fairway.

The pallbearers were professionals, but they waited at the grave with the three of us, to make it look less lonely.

And then, just as the minister began to drop his handful of dirt onto the coffin below, there was a shout of "Fore!" from the thirteenth tee.

Some dub had really sliced his drive. I was facing the tee; I saw the ball coming, and ducked.

The ball bounced twice—and rolled into the grave. I heard a hollow "thump" as it hit the coffin . . .

Praise for Brock Callahan

Charter Books by William Campbell Gault

MURDER IN THE RAW

William Campbell Gault

(Previously Published in Hardcover as *Ring Around Rosa*)

CHARTER BOOKS, NEW YORK

This book was published in
hardcover by Dutton as *Ring Around Rosa*.

This Charter Book contains the complete
text of the original edition.

MURDER IN THE RAW

A Charter Book / published by arrangement with
the author

PRINTING HISTORY
Dutton edition published 1955
Previously published by Dell Books
Charter edition / August 1988

ISBN: 1-55773-061-X

Charter Books are published by The Berkley Publishing Group,
200 Madison Avenue, New York, New York 10016.
The name "CHARTER" and the "C" logo are trademarks
belonging to Charter Communications, Inc.

PRINTED IN THE UNITED STATES OF AMERICA

10   9   8   7   6   5   4   3   2   1

THERE IS an old gridiron wheeze that states a guard is only a fullback with his brains knocked out. I have met some rather bright guards and some extremely stupid fullbacks, but what is a fact measured against the generality?

I'd played a few years of guard, myself, the more prominent years with the Rams and made a lot of friends in Los Angeles. So it figured that when the boys began to clobber me, Los Angeles was the logical place to open up a business.

Beverly Hills is not Los Angeles, however. Beverly Hills is the most vigorously policed area in the nation and opening up an investigative agency in that smug little suburb is really carrying coal to Newcastle. So that supports the generality.

But I had friends in the town and three years in the O.S.S. My old man had been a cop and I knew every Ram fan on the L.A.P.D. There are a hell of a lot of them. And in Beverly Hills, on South Beverly Drive, I found the "neatest little pine-paneled office you ever saw at a shamefully low rental." That description is the realtor's and almost accurate, so I gave him the first month's shameful rental, and bought some furniture.

And I sat and waited.

Sitting and waiting, I imagined who my first client would be. A banker, gray at the temples, with a wife twenty years younger and fifty pounds lighter? Some luscious young widow who was beginning to have doubts about an oily and debonair suitor? Some millionaire sportsman whose son was in trouble?

Who would walk in?

Juan Mira walked in.

If you live in this area, you will remember Juan Mira. He won more fights than he lost, but he lost a lot of them. The marks of all the fights are on the broad, flat face of Juan Mira.

At the Olympic, he had always been a crowd pleaser. And outside of the ring, his reputation was that he was also a woman pleaser. Most Filipinos try to be; it is a serious business with them.

Juan stood about five-four and would now weigh about a hundred and thirty. He wore a neat and creamy tropical weave suit and white buck shoes and a big-brimmed leghorn hat with an extremely colorful band. There are not many Miras in Beverly Hills; Juan was really out of his element.

"I know your name," he said. "I see you play."

"With the Rams?" I asked, a stupid question.

He nodded. "With the Rams. Best damn guard in the business."

"Thank you, Juan," I said. "I've seen you fight." I searched my memory. "You looked mighty good against Carmine Padro."

Juan nodded, and his eyes were reminiscent. "I could always handle Carmine. Which Padro fight you see?"

"The one where you knocked him out in the sixth," I said. "At the Olympic."

He nodded, and sighed. He took a gold cigarette case out of an inside jacket pocket and offered me an ivory-tipped cigarette, which I refused.

I gestured toward a chair. "You didn't come here to talk football or fights, Juan. Sit down and tell me your troubles."

He sat down and lighted the cigarette with a slim, platinum lighter. He blew sweet-smelling smoke out into the room and said, "It's about my girl. Rosa is her name. She's gone."

"Gone—? How do you mean, gone?"

"From her place, where she lives." He snapped his fingers. "One day she is there. Next day, no Rosa."

"Does she work? Did you check her place of employment?"

"She works. Sing a little, dance a little. Not working lately." He shook his head. "Night clubs—slow."

"Not all over," I suggested. "Maybe she got a job in another town. Say—Las Vegas?"

He shook his head. "Not Rosa. Small clubs for Rosa. She is no big-time operator."

Small, *cheap* clubs. A stripper, probably. I said, "Were you so close you'd expect her to tell you if she left town?"

"We are engaged," Juan said with dignity.

"How long, Juan?" I asked.

He looked at me doubtfully. "Two years."

"And she never went out with another man in those two years?"

His eyes were hard and shiny. "So—? What kind of question is that?"

"Maybe she went off with another man, now," I said.

"Easy, Mr. Callahan," he said.

"You don't know that she didn't, do you?"

"I know Rosa. She play around a little. But she don't walk out on Juan, not Rosa. I treat her like a—a *queen*." He clenched a fist.

"I see. What did the police say about it? You've given all this to Missing Persons, I suppose?"

He frowned. "No. Don't you want my business?"

I shook my head. "I'm not Dorothy Dix, Juan. You two had a quarrel, didn't you? And she walked out on you. And you want to pay me to drag her back."

He took a deep breath. He reached over and crushed out his cigarette in the ash tray on my desk. He said, *"No!"*

Silence in the pine-paneled office with the low rent. Then Juan stood up and looked down at me. "To hell with you. You're so big, huh? You don't need Filipino money. Big, Beverly Hills bastard, Brock Callahan. To hell with you, again."

He stood erectly, glaring at me, dignified and ferocious.

I said soothingly, "Don't ruffle your tail feathers, Juan. It's just that I don't want to cheat you. Do you want to pay me sixty dollars a day to look for her? How much of that could you take?"

His voice was ice. "You think I'm poor? Because I don't live in Beverly Hills, you think I'm nothing. Don't worry about Juan Mira."

He took out an alligator billfold and removed three crisp, new bills. He tossed them contemptuously onto the desk. Hundred dollar bills.

If he left here, he'd go somewhere else. He might go to one of the big reputable agencies, but the chances were he'd go to one of the small, disreputable agencies. And he *was* my first client.

I said, "Sit down, Juan, and tell me about her."

He told me about her. She was Portuguese, Filipino and Chinese and her name was Rosa Carmona. He had two pictures of her, one a head and one a full-length, theatrical portrait of her in spangles and not much else.

Her face was round and there was a trace of slant to the merry brown eyes. Her figure was rounded and not so plump it would displease any reasonable man. For a man with a face like Juan Mira's she would be an exceptionally lucky catch.

"Very pretty," I said.

"Hmmmm," he said, which could have meant anything.

"What was her last place of employment?"

"Chico's," he said. "That's in Culver City."

"And before that?"

He named some other places in Culver City, Santa Monica and Venice. None of them were places I'd ever heard of, but I was no booze hound.

I put it all down in my neat script and said, "Okay, Juan, I'll keep in touch with you."

He rose and smiled. "I am sorry about before. You are no bastard, Brock Callahan. Best damn guard in the business."

"Thank you," I said, again. "And you looked mighty good against Carmine Padro."

He nodded, and held a fist aloft, and went out the door, trying not to walk on his heels.

Out at Redlands, my old buddies were working under that baking sun, getting ready for the *Times* charity game with the Redskins that always opened the season for us.

In my little office, there was just a tinge of smog coming through the open window. And my bad right knee told me there was some moisture in the air. I'd had the torn cartilage removed and the knee no longer locked on me. But it ached on damp days.

I looked at the photographs of Rosa Carmona and could guess she had one of those smooth, dark and hair-free bodies the boys on Oahu could never seem to get enough of.

The bills looked newly minted. I made out a deposit slip and took them around to the bank. Then I climbed into the flivver and drove out to Culver City.

It was an hour before noon and there was a chance the place wasn't open yet. I could have phoned, but I was getting awful sick of sitting around that office.

In front of Chico's, an eight-foot color cutout depicted the fine long legs and feminine bumps of "Billie Brent—

The Girl Who Invented The Sensational Zipper Flipper. You'll Flip Your Lid When She Unzips What's Hid."

For Culver City, this was mild, institutional-type advertising.

Inside Chico's, a swamper was wearily mopping the asphalt tile floor. The chairs were on the tables and the odors of detergent and stale beer fought an air war to a stalemate.

Behind the bar in the small barroom to my left, a thin, sour-looking man in a white shirt was carefully arranging the bottles of watered whiskey.

"We're not open yet," he told me. "How'd you get in?"

"Through the big room. I'm not a customer. I'm making a check." I put the mildest of my business cards on the bar, the one that read, *Credit Investigations*.

He looked at it and yawned. "Checking who?"

"A girl named Rosa Carmona. This was her last place of employment so far as we know."

He nodded. "She worked here. Hot little bundle of mama, that one. Biggest attraction we ever had. She wasn't afraid to put on a show, that Rosa." He gestured toward the bigger room. "Most of these tramps are phonies."

"But you let her go, just the same, eh?"

"Not me. I'm not the boss. I just work here, Mac. What queered Rosa here was that boy friend of hers. Jealous little bastard. Maybe you remember him—Juan Mira?"

I frowned. "I think so. Wasn't he a fighter?"

"Yeh—one of those bums that used to be so big at the Olympic. Club fighter, going nowhere, but real big among his own kind, I guess."

"Filipino, isn't he?"

"That's right. And jealous as hell. Used to come in here, just waiting for some guy to make a dirty crack during Rosa's show. We had to bounce him a couple times. Felony, you know, for a fighter to use his fists outside the ring in this state."

I nodded. "So Juan really queered the kid, huh?"

"Sure. Little bastard—"

"You don't know where Rosa went from here, then?"

He shook his head. "I don't, Mac. Didn't she say, when she applied for credit?"

I said easily. "She applied for the credit when she was working here. And she got it. Now, some bills are due, and we're trying to find her."

"Oh. Well, your best bet would be Mira. He's probably got her set up some place."

"Thanks," I said. "I'll check that. Could I buy you a drink?"

He shook his head. "Never touch it."

From Culver City to Santa Monica and from Santa Monica to Venice. Nothing in Santa Monica, but in Venice, on Windward Avenue, the bartender referred me to a bleached and battered blonde going over some sheet music with the piano player.

The blonde bore a faint resemblance to the picture in the window advertising—"Sue Ellen, the Savannah Songbird."

"Sue Ellen," I said, "I understand you're a friend of Rosa Carmona's."

"I know her. So?"

"I thought you might know where I could find her." I handed her the credit investigation card.

Sue Ellen looked at the card for seconds. When she looked up again, her eyes were blanker than usual. "Something wrong with her credit?"

"Just routine checking," I said in my Dragnet best. "Her credit seems to have been excellent up until recently.

Now, there are a few bills due, and Miss Carmona has left no forwarding address."

"You're no credit man," Sue Ellen said. "Credit men don't talk about due bills. What's the pitch, Buster?"

"I've explained it to you," I said. "You're not compelled to answer, of course."

"No kidding——? Take off, Buster. I know who you're working for, that punchy little Mira. Breeze, man, you're in enemy country."

I shrugged. "All right. When you see Miss Carmona, though, I wish you would have her phone me at the number on that card. One's credit is very important, today, you know."

"Blow," Sue Ellen said. "Good-by. Don't hurry back."

I shook my head. "You certainly don't sound like Savannah to me, Miss Sue Ellen. You needn't be crude."

The piano player got up from his bench, studied me—and sat down again. The bartender gave a lot of attention to the glass he was polishing.

I gave them all my broad back and went out into the sea-tinged air of Windward Avenue. I drove from there to Rosa's last place of residence, a triplex on Barrington. It was a neat and colorful place of brown stucco and chartreuse trim. The flower beds were edged neatly along the perfect lawn and bougainvillaea covered the front wall of the landlady's apartment.

Rosa, she told me, had been paid up until the first of the month, but hadn't given the proper month's notice. She had left two evenings before, to the best of the landlady's knowledge.

She sniffed. "That—that wrestler person, that friend or whatever, thought that Miss Carmona might be ill or—or worse, as she hadn't answered her phone or doorbell. So I used my master key and we saw that she had taken all her clothes. The furniture is mine, of course."

"You don't mean 'wrestler,' do you? You mean Juan Mira, the boxer?"

"That's the man."

"Did Miss Carmona have other friends?"

"I'm sure I don't know, Mr.—" she looked at my card "—Callahan. I don't check on my tenants' social life."

"And Miss Carmona left no forwarding address, not even with the mailman?"

"None. The mailman told me that only this morning."

I thanked her and went back to the flivver. Where now? All the places Juan had named, I had checked. And where now? I headed back toward Beverly Hills.

It was after two o'clock and I had eaten no lunch. I put my car on the lot, and walked over to the drugstore for their special of the day—beef stew.

Out on Beverly Drive, the local Cadillacs moved impatiently around the cheaper, transient cars. In the drugstore, the big fan overhead turned lazily and the malt mixers whirred and the fat woman on the stool next to mine slowly turned the pages of *Vogue,* while she spooned into a hot fudge sundae with marshmallow topping.

The counterman said, "How's it going, Brock? I'll bet you're sorry you're not out there at Redlands with the boys, huh?"

"It must be hot in Redlands," I said. "I'll take the beef stew. And some of those rye rolls if there are any left."

He winked at me. "I figured you'd be in. I saved you a couple."

The Rams are well loved in L.A.

The fat lady looked at me briefly and quizzically but evidently couldn't identify me as a movie, stage, radio, TV or night-club star. She went back to her *Vogue* and hot fudge.

She left before I'd finished my beef stew, and the counter-man shook his head as he watched her waddle over to the cashier. "Now we have a nice hot fudge and marshmallow stained *Vogue* to sell. These rich old broads kill me. They buy a sundae and read seven magazines and put them back."

"Maybe she's not a rich old broad," I said. "Maybe she's a tourist from Westwood."

"That's pretty good," he said. "Maybe you should have worked up a night-club act. More butter, Brock?"

He always called me by my first name, though I never did learn either of his. I ate the beef stew and drank a cup of coffee and went up the steps to my office.

My phone answering service told me there had been no calls. I got out some forms and began to type up the reports on my calls for the day. It was slow going on my hunt and peck system. I was about half through when the phone rang.

"Meester Brock Callahan?"

"This is he."

"This is Rosa Carmona. Why you want me?"

"A friend of yours is looking for you, Miss Carmona," I explained. "He is very worried about you."

"So, you lied, eh? You said I owe money. You told my friend I owe money. You leave me alone, Meester Callahan. And you tell Juan Mira to leave me alone. I don't want to see him, *Ever!*"

"Juan loves you very much, Rosa," I said gently. "Don't send his ring back until he's had a chance to talk to you."

"Ring? He wants the ring? I'll give him——He got plenty from me for that ring. He wants his ring?"

It had just been a bit of phraseology, but I said, "Why don't you bring it to the office, here, and we can talk this out? You and Juan have been sweethearts a long time, you know."

"Too long," she said. "I'll keep the ring." The line went dead.

I phoned Juan Mira at the number he had left with me. Juan answered, and I told him about Rosa's call.

"Where is she?" he asked excitedly. "Where did she call from?"

"I don't know, Juan. She doesn't want to see you any more. She said she wouldn't send your ring back."

"Never mind. You keep looking for her. You will find her. Maybe she is with that blonde whore from Venice."

"Sue Ellen?"

"She is the one. You go to her place."

"Juan, *no!* I am not Dorothy Dix, as I told you. Rosa doesn't want to see you and that's her right. I can't force her to see you."

Silence, and then, "Please, Mr. Callahan, you keep looking? It is so very important to Juan. And do not worry about money. There is plenty."

I said wearily, "If she phones again, I'll let you know, Juan. But I couldn't charge you for full-time service every day. There's no place to look; you'd be cheated."

"You keep looking," he said, and hung up.

I went back to typing up the report. Juan wouldn't want one, but I had decided to make reports on everything, for my own files. It gave me a sense of business efficiency and killed the long, waiting hours.

Outside, a Jaguar snorted and a hot-rod snorted back in contempt. The breeze shifted to its afternoon westerly and blew the flimsy carbon papers from the desk.

I bent over to pick them up and the wind blew one under the love seat against the wall. I was on my knees in front of that, reaching for it, when my door opened.

I saw two pair of feet, and looked up to see two faces frowning at me. Both the feet and the faces were stamped "Cop."

"You Brock Callahan?" one of them asked, and I nodded.

Silence for a second, and I asked, "Well, what's up, gentlemen?"

"Murder," one of them said.

CHAPTER TWO

I STOOD UP and dusted off my hands. "Someone I know?" I asked quietly,

"You tell us. His name is Roger Scott."

"Never heard of him," I said. I went back to the desk and put the sheets of carbon paper very carefully atop the pile and put a paperweight on top of that. I went over to my chair and sat down. The two men just looked at me.

I said, "I suppose you two are police officers? Beverly Hills?"

The one who had done the talking shook his head. He was a broad man and fairly tall with a surprisingly thin, bloodhound's face. The other man was shorter and fatter, but not nearly as broad.

The taller one said, "I'm Sergeant Pascal, and this is Officer Caroline. Didn't you play tackle for the Rams?"

"Guard," I said. "Are you gentlemen from the West Los Angeles Station?"

"That's right. When's the last time you saw Roger Scott?"

"I never heard of him," I protested.

"Don't lie to us, Callahan," Caroline said. "He phoned you, from that Brentwood motel, just one hour ago."

I shook my head. "I came into the office about an hour and a half ago. My phone answering service will confirm that I had no calls up to then. And I've had one incoming call since, from a girl named Rosa Carmona."

Pascal looked at Caroline and nodded. "A girl. That's the way it was. That manager just puts down the number called and the number of the unit calling. That's all the slip showed."

Pascal turned back to me. "Where's this Rosa Carmona now? And where'd she call from?"

"I don't know where she is, now, and I don't know where she phoned from," I said. "She phoned about an hour ago."

Caroline started to say something, but Pascal put a hand on his arm. Then Pascal said quietly, "Suppose you give us the whole picture, Callahan? Start right from the beginning and don't miss anything."

Caroline put his fat body down onto the love seat and Pascal came over to sit in my customer's chair.

I leaned back in my office chair, like those private eyes do in the movies, and gave them the whole picture in a restrained and well modulated voice.

Pascal had a notebook out and when I finished, he picked up the phone on my desk. He called the station, and gave them the address and phone number Juan had given me. "Pick him up," he said. "We're on the way in, now, with another one."

He replaced the phone and looked at me. "C'mon, Dick Tracy. Time's a'wasting."

"What's the charge?" I asked.

Pascal smiled at his buddy and looked back at me. "No charge. Come on."

The pudgy Caroline stood up. "Want me to drag him out, Sarge?"

"You put a hand on me, lard-ass," I told him, "and I'll throw you right through that window, there. And if you don't think I can, start something."

Caroline's soft face stiffened and he put a hand in under his jacket.

Pascal said sharply, "All right, Pudge, take it easy." He looked back at me. "Who the hell do you think you are?"

"A private operative with a Beverly Hills office," I said evenly. "And if you'd like me to phone the Chief, here, I'm sure he'd give me a character reference. Or you could call your own station and ask Captain Apoyan about me, or Lieutenant Trask."

Caroline looked at Pascal. Pascal looked at me, and shook his head. "Name-dropper, eh? All right, Mr. Callahan, would you kindly accompany us to the West Side Station where we can continue our previous conversation? Your client will be there, and we can iron everything out."

On the way down the steps, Pascal was chuckling. At the bottom, he said, "You sounded very tough upstairs, there, Callahan. It's too bad you couldn't have been that tough against the Forty-niners, last season. They sure made a patsy out of you."

"Your memory's bad," I told him. "They didn't gain a yard through my position."

Juan was at the West Side Station when we arrived. He was in a room with barred windows, talking to a detective. A uniformed man was taking notes. The plain-clothes man turned around, and I saw that it was Lieutenant Trask.

"Brock—," he said. "Brock the Rock—what the hell brings you in here this fine day?"

"Pascal and Caroline," I said. "How are you, Dave?"

"Surprised." He looked at Pascal. "Callahan in some sort of trouble, Sergeant?"

Pascal shrugged. "He might be. Somebody phoned him from that motel room where Scott was killed."

"Phoned Brock—?" He looked back at Juan and then again at me. "Oh, that's right—you're a private investigator now, aren't you? I remember reading about it." He smiled. "Juan didn't want to give me your name. What's the story, Brock?"

The uniformed man turned his notebook to a blank page and looked questioningly at the lieutenant. Trask's nod was almost imperceptible.

Pascal said casually, "Maybe we'd better get their stories *separately*, Lieutenant."

Annoyance on Trask's face and then he nodded. "A good idea. Caroline, take Mira out into the hall until we call you. Away from the door."

Caroline took Mira from the room and Dave Trask indicated a chair. "Sit down, Callahan, and tell us about it."

I had gone from "Brock" to "Callahan" in less than a minute. A cop is a cop is a cop. I gave it to him, just as I had to Pascal and Caroline and the uniformed man took it all down.

When I'd finished, Trask looked at the sergeant. "That manager didn't say anything about a woman being in the room, did he?"

Pascal shook his head. "But if they cut the hot pillow trade away from those Brentwood motels, they'd all go out of business, Lieutenant. It figures the manager wouldn't mention a woman. I guess we'd better lean on him a little, don't you think?"

Trask nodded, and looked at me. "We'll get this typed up, and you can sign it. Wait out in the hall until we talk to Mira."

Pascal went to the door, and beckoned the others in. My client didn't look at me as we passed. His eyes were on the floor, as though he were getting prefight instructions from the referee.

Nobody came out to the hall with me; evidently I wasn't as seriously involved as their manner had suggested. I sat on a bench out there, studying the opposite wall.

In a little while, Pascal came to the door to gesture me back into the room. The uniformed man went out as I came in.

Lieutenant Dave Trask waved me to a chair. "Sit and relax, Brock. We'll be ready with those statements in a few minutes."

I sat down, pleased to hear I was again Brock. Caroline went out and Pascal went over to stand near the barred window. Juan Mira looked at me anxiously from his seat near the desk.

I smiled at him and held a clenched fist up.

Trask said, "You say, Brock, that Rosa Carmona phoned you. But you're not sure of that, are you?"

"I only know she said she was Rosa Carmona. I never heard her voice before."

"She have an accent?"

"Some. It could have been faked. As a matter of fact, looking back on it, I don't think it was consistent."

Mira frowned. "Consistent—? What you mean, consistent?"

I turned to him. "I mean, Juan, that I didn't think she used an accent all the time. It was like she could turn it off and on."

Juan nodded. "She does. For her shows, accent. No show, no accent."

"Easy, Juan," I said. "You're putting her in the grease. Maybe it wasn't Rosa, at all. Maybe it was somebody trying to frame her."

"Maybe who would that be?" Trask asked quietly.

"I don't know," I said. "That's for the police to find out."

Trask smiled. "All right, Brock. Let's not be bitter. You're new to this business. You've got a lot to learn."

I said nothing.

Trask said, "One thing you learned today is to stay very far away from any homicide cases. We don't like private investigators getting involved in those."

I said nothing.

Mira said softly, "You still look for my Rosa, Brock? You find her for me?"

"Ten thousand cops will be looking for her, Juan," I told him. "For free."

He made a face. "Cops—! Stinking crooks, cops. Yellow bellies, cops."

From the window, Pascal said, "Easy, little man. Watch your language."

Juan stood up, his slight body trembling. "Little man? One hundred thirty-five pounds. You want to fight this little man, yellow belly?"

"Sit down, Juan," I said. "Sit down and shut up, or I'll fight you. You can't lick city hall, Juan."

He glared at me for a moment, and then sat down. Pascal said softly, "Oh, those Forty-niners—"

I said to Trask, "Tell that Monday morning quarterback at the window the Forty-niners never ran over me."

Trask nodded. "I'll confirm that. How come you got into this private eye dodge, Brock? Things can't be that rough."

"I have a natural talent for it," I told him. "My old man was a cop, you might remember."

"That's right. I'd forgotten. In Dago, wasn't it?"

I nodded.

"You might have tried the Department, Brock. We need men desperately."

"I can guess that by what I've seen today," I agreed. "To use your own words, things aren't that rough."

Pascal came over from his position at the window. His bloodhound's face was pale. "Do I have to take that kind of crap, Lieutenant?"

Trask looked down at the desk top. Juan Mira smiled. I said, "I'll apologize, Sergeant, if you'll promise to get off that Forty-niner kick. We *all* have our pride, you know."

Pascal muttered something, and went out the door.

Dave Trask said gravely, "You're getting a bad start in

your profession, Brock. You can use friends, just like anyone else."

"I'm a friendly man, by nature," I answered honestly. "But I never learned to swallow insolence and I don't intend to learn now."

Trask sighed. Outside, there was the screech of brakes and a shouted curse. Juan Mira took out the gold cigarette case and removed one of the ivory-tipped cigarettes. His slim, platinum lighter flashed in a ray coming through the Venetian blinds.

Trask watched him and shook his head. He looked at me and shrugged. Time crawled by.

Then the uniformed man was coming back into the room with our statements. Mira's was read to him; I read my own. We both signed them.

Then I asked, "How do I get back to Beverly Hills?"

Trask frowned and looked at the uniformed man.

Juan said, "I take you, Brock. My car is here."

It was one of those salmon-colored new Merc convertibles, complete with everything but a lemon slicer. The twin pipes murmured mellowly to each other as he gunned over toward Wilshire.

"Souped?" I asked him.

He nodded. "Heads and carbs and pipes. Enough for Juan. Too much for Rosa. Rosa like the big fat cars."

"You may never see Rosa again, Juan," I said. "She may be a long way from here by now."

"You find her," he said confidently. "I pay you and you find her."

The Merc moved in and out of the traffic stream, about two hundred horses under the command of a hundred and thirty-five pound giant. At the light on Barclay, a Cad driver looked over and gunned his motor in anticipation.

With the green, the Merc jumped, her tires squealing.

We were half a block away before the Cad could get out of the intersection. The smell of burning rubber came up to us as we slowed.

"Easy, Juan," I said. "We've got all the trouble with the law we can handle right now."

"Cops—" Juan said, and spit out at the windstream.

I chuckled. "We're citizens, now, Juan. We are no longer prominent sports figures with free tickets to hand out. We had better learn to get along with the law."

He didn't answer that. He drove without further dialogue all the way to my office. There, he double-parked while I climbed out.

Then he said, "You find my Rosa," and the Merc went gunning off, her tail pipes seeming to mock me.

CHAPTER THREE

THE MORNING papers gave it a front-page splash, including a subhead in the *Times* about *Ex-Ram Star Questioned In Motel Murder.* There was a picture of me in Ram uniform in the *Times* and somehow they managed to drag in the coming Ram-Redskin Times Charity Game. In this paper, Roger Scott was identified as an author.

In the *Daily News,* I was identified as a former football player now turned private investigator. Roger Scott was called a writer and literary agent. In southern California, and particularly in this area, any unemployed person identifies himself as a writer. It seems to be the standard excuse for idleness. There was a picture of Roger Scott in the *News* and unless it was a completely doctored portrait, he had been a very handsome man in the Barrymore tradition.

There was no mention of Rosa Carmona by name. The police were sitting on that. There was mention in the *News* of a "mystery woman" threading through the case. I could imagine what the afternoon Hearst paper would make of that one.

The *Daily News* also mentioned a "prominent former pugilist" being involved but again he was unnamed. Too many people knew Juan Mira was engaged to Rosa; too many of Rosa's friends knew that.

Roger Scott had been knifed to death. There were fourteen stab wounds in his body and throat.

I had read it all and worked my way to the sport pages when my office door opened.

A girl stood there, a fairly tall girl with onyx hair in an Italian haircut, a beautiful girl. She wore a lime-colored

27

shantung suit, rather primly cut, but no suit would make her look like anything but *all* woman.

She was not alone. Behind her, there was a young man who could have been seventeen or twenty-one. He had an adolescent moodiness in his finely featured face. He was taller than the girl and a lot broader.

The girl asked, "Mr. Brock Callahan?"

I rose, and nodded.

She smiled rather stiffly. "I'm Glenys Christopher. This is my brother, Bobby. He *had* to come along to meet you."

"How do you do?" I said, and then the name of Bobby Christopher rang a bell in my mind. I asked, "Not *the* Bobby Christopher?"

He had been an All-State halfback at Beverly Hills High School. He had played with the South in the annual North-South prep star game.

The lad smiled. "Yes, sir. That's why I wanted to shake your hand. I think you're the greatest guard the Rams ever had."

He came over to shake my hand and I thought I could dimly hear a trumpet flare.

"Thank you," I said. "From what I've read, you play a lot of football yourself. Going to S.C. this fall, are you?"

"I haven't decided, yet," he told me. "I'm—weighing the offers."

His sister said quietly, "Now, that the formalities are over, Bobby, would you wait in the car?" Her voice was strained.

"Sure thing," he said, and grinned and waved. He closed the door behind him.

I gestured to my customer's chair. "Business brought you here, Miss Christopher?"

She nodded, frowning. She sat erectly in the pull-up chair.

I went over to sit behind my desk, again. She took out

a package of cigarettes from her purse and offered me one.

I shook my head. "Thank you. I don't smoke." I flipped my desk lighter into flame for her. She leaned forward and the light from the window behind me glowed on her lustrous black hair.

She sat erectly again and thanked me and I nodded. Finally, she said, "I don't know exactly where to begin."

"The beginning's as good a place as any." I had learned that from Sergeant Pascal, yesterday.

She took a deep breath and looked at my desk top. "Well, to begin with—I was in love with Roger Scott." She looked paler. "We—weren't engaged—officially, that is, but—" She took another breath and leaned forward to crush out her newly lighted cigarette in my ash tray.

I couldn't think of anything to say.

She sat stiffly erect once more and looked at me beseechingly. "I'm frightened, Mr. Callahan."

"I could guess that," I said quietly. "Are you frightened of the person who—killed Roger Scott?"

She nodded. "Mostly—" She looked down at her hands in her lap. "Do you know, do the police know who killed him?"

"*I* don't know. I'm not sure about the police. Do you know?"

She looked up, startled. "Of course not. How could I?"

"I wondered why you were here."

"If I knew," she said softly, "I would have gone to the police. It's—it's Roger's background I want investigated."

"Why?"

She looked at me defiantly. "My—friends didn't think much of him. And now this has happened and there's this horrible rumor about some—woman being involved, and —" She put a hand on the desk. "Don't you see? I want to *know* about him."

"Rumors can't touch him," I said gently. "Not now.

And the police will be looking very thoroughly into his background. They have more facilities for a search like that than I have. You'd be spending your money for a doubtful service, Miss Christopher."

Her face was white. "I'm not concerned with money. And you, obviously, don't want my patronage." She rose. "Could you tell me why?"

"Please, hear me out, Miss Christopher," I said. "You are the second client I've had in my short investigative career. The first one walked in here yesterday morning. That's what involved me in the death of Mr. Scott. I was warned, yesterday, by the Los Angeles Police Department to stay very far away from any murder case. I would hate to start out on the wrong side of the fence from *them*."

She stared at me for seconds. "I have to have someone to turn to, Mr. Callahan. Bobby and I are alone in the world. And he thought *so much* of you. And then, when we read you were involved, somehow, in this, it seemed liked a stroke of luck, in a way, almost—" She stopped and shook her head annoyedly. "I'm sorry. I'm being a pest." She nodded, and turned toward the door.

"Wait," I said.

She stopped, and turned back.

"Sit down," I said, "and tell me about Roger Scott."

It was all standard enough. She had met him at a Hollywood party. He was amusing, he was handsome and that was enough for the first attraction. Later, she learned he was also sensitive and talented and bitter. And broke.

She looked beyond me. "My friends got pathological about him. I don't know why they should take such an interest in my affairs, but I was constantly being warned about him. They considered him a fortune hunter and a fraud."

"So now you want to know if they were right about him?"

"I'd like to prove them wrong. But I want to know the truth."

"Why?"

"You asked me that, before," she said. "Isn't it enough that I want to know and I'm willing to pay to find out?"

"It should be enough for me," I admitted. "My rent is due this week. What surprises me is that you didn't have him investigated *before* he died."

"Would you have someone you love investigated?"

"If I were wealthy enough to attract a fortune hunter, I certainly would. This is a community property state, Miss Christopher."

She looked at me coldly. "I wasn't interested in his friends before—yesterday. But now I am—and I'm frightened. I guess we're right back where we started, aren't we, Mr. Callahan?"

"Not quite," I said. "I'll check him for you. Two days should handle it. I'm working on another case, now, but they may be related." I paused. "And if they are, I guess that would make it illegal to work on both of them."

She said quickly, "Related—? In what way?"

"I can't tell you any more than the newspapers have. You came to me, didn't you, because of the newspaper stories?"

"Partly," she said. "But mostly because of Bobby. He thinks you're some kind of—god."

"He must be the first halfback in the history of the game to admire a guard," I told her. "But thank you. And I'll report to you as soon as I get anything substantial."

She stood up, "Thank *you*, Mr. Callahan." She went out, leaving the faintest tinge of her fragrance behind.

Below, at the curb, Bobby waited in an Austin-Healey. From above, the car looked low enough for the driver to drag his hand on the pavement. The lime-colored shantung suit came into view from the building entrance below, and Bobby reached over to open the door for his sister.

Even from this view, she was compellingly attractive, a flame for any vagrant moth. Add a few dollars and you had a package eagerly sought for in towns far less predatory than this one. Name me a man not attracted by beauty *and* money, *name me one.*

Where do you check an author? The Screen Writers' Guild had no record of any screen credits for Roger Scott. The Authors' Guild was not active in this area. The MWA's local vice-president had never heard of him, but he promised to check with New York.

He had also been a literary agent, and I found him in the phone book under that listing. The office was in Hollywood.

It was a white stucco building on Vine Street, and the office of *Roger Scott, Literary Agent* was not closed.

A young man sat at a typewriter in the inner office and he was clacking away at a phenomenal speed. I stood in the doorway from the outer office, watching him. The noise of his typing had prevented him from hearing the hall door open; I studied the room.

There were four desks in the room, but only one of them was occupied. Manila manuscript envelopes, unopened, were piled on two of the desks.

I said, "Business must be good."

The flying fingers stopped, and he looked at me, startled.

"I guess you didn't hear the outer door open," I said.

He nodded, studying me. "I guess I didn't. How can I help you, sir?" He took a cigarette from a package on the desk and lighted it.

I came farther into the room. "You can tell me about Roger Scott."

He inhaled deeply and looked at me curiously. "He's

dead. We were partners. Could I ask why you are interested in him?"

"My name is Brock Callahan. I'm a private investigator. I'm working for a client who is interested in the reason for Scott's death."

The young man stood up, and I saw that he was tall, as well as thin. He threw his shoulders back and took a deep breath and massaged his neck muscles with a long-fingered hand. The first two fingers of his right hand were yellowish-brown with tobacco stain.

"Sit down if you want," he said. "The police have already gone over Rog's history with a magnifying glass. He was twenty-eight years old, six feet tall. I suppose he could be called handsome. He had three books published."

I sat down on a straight-backed chair. "You were his partner, you say. The listing in the phone book and on the board downstairs seems to indicate it was Roger Scott's business."

"It was under his name. To be candid with you, I did 80 per cent of the work. But Rog founded the agency. He's dead, now, and I intend to carry it on."

"I see. Who published his books?"

The thin man's smile was wry. "A firm by the name of Studio Press. We like to call them a cooperative publishing house. Some cynics use the term 'vanity press' but we don't encourage it among our clients."

"I'm not following you," I said.

He sighed. "It's very simple. You are a hopeful author and you want someone to publish your book, naturally. So all you have to do is pay for it, and firms like *Studio Press* will publish your book."

"I see. And then the author can hope that he will make enough on the book to cover his publication expenses."

"He can and does. Not that it matters too much, though.

He *does* have a published book, doesn't he? There's some prestige in that, isn't there?"

"I suppose," I said. "What Roger Scott wanted was prestige, then?"

"I'm not sure. All three of those books were published before I met him. They were published before he opened this agency."

"From the looks of things," I said, "the agency is doing a fine business."

He frowned. "From the looks of what things?"

"All those scripts you haven't opened, yet. Was that just today's mail?"

He nodded. "There's another thing you might not understand. This is an agency that advertises for clients, looks for clients. And we charge a reading fee to amateurs. We charge them for what we call an analysis. In our profession, we occupy about the same position that advertising dentists and physicians do in their's."

"That's frank enough," I said. "Quack is the word, isn't it?"

He looked at me levelly. "To some. I figure I do all these amateurs a lot of good. I've brought a few of them to important sales. I'm not ashamed."

"Was Roger Scott?"

"I don't know. He was cynical. I honestly don't know how much conscience he had."

"Maybe he was killed by a disgruntled client," I said.

"I've no idea."

"He's been described to me as sensitive and talented and bitter and broke."

"He was bitter. Maybe he was sensitive; I'm not sensitive enough to judge. He wasn't talented and only a wealthy person would consider him broke."

"My client is a wealthy person."

"I can imagine. A wealthy, feminine person. Rog knew a lot of them."

"I've heard him described as a fortune hunter and a fraud, too," I continued.

The thin young man shrugged. "That's opinion and one man's is as good as another's."

Silence, for a few seconds, and then I asked, "What's your name?"

"Joe," he said, "Joe Kramer. Why?"

"I don't know. I suppose a competent investigator would ask that first. I'm new at this racket."

Kramer smiled. "I'm fairly new at this one. I hope we both make out, don't you?"

I stood up. "I do. You seem to have a good start. Anything else you can tell me about Scott?"

"He gambled some. Maybe he didn't pay off. What the hell he was doing at that motel, we can only guess about. We'd probably both guess the same thing if your mind is as dirty as mine."

I nodded. "And who were his best friends, male and female?"

Kramer shook his head. "I can't help you much there. I didn't travel in his set. There was a girl named Glenys, one of those Beverly Hills bombs and some new one—I forgot her name. She was an actress or singer, or something—"

"Rosa?" I asked. "Rosa Carmona?"

"That's it. The rest of Rog's friends were just some names I've forgotten now. If any of them drop in, do you want me to keep a list of their names for you?"

"I'd appreciate it. Thanks a lot, Joe."

He smiled. "Don't mention it. Any time you work up a salable script, bring it in; I'll read it for a fin."

The typewriter was clacking again by the time I got to the door.

Outside, we had a lot of sun and no smog. The seat of my flivver was warm and the steering wheel was hot. I tooled it through the late morning Sunset traffic to Kenmore and turned left, to a six-unit apartment building.

There was an elderly man trimming the hedge that bordered the sidewalk here. He wore khaki dungarees, held up by faded elastic suspenders, and a blue work shirt. He wore a stained panama hat and an air of disinterest in the work he was doing.

I told him who I was and asked him if he'd known Roger Scott.

"Should," he said. "Tenant of mine. You got anything to chew on you?"

I shook my head.

"Even a cigarette?" he asked. "I can chew 'em. The old lady won't give me a dime for tobacco, not a dime."

"Here's a half," I said. "Buy some tobacco."

He looked at me coldly. "I'm no panhandler, mister. I own this apartment building."

"I know," I said. "And this half dollar isn't mine. It will go onto the bill of my client. Do you know where Scott lived before he lived here?"

He didn't answer. He kept looking at the half dollar, still in my hand. Then he glanced toward the house. Lady Nicotine won another one. He took the coin and nodded his thanks.

He set the long clippers atop the stiff hedge. "Let's sit in the shade. That sun's murder today."

There were some redwood chairs in the shade of a huge parasol, and we walked over and sat down. There, he said, "Cops have been here, asking about Roger. The old lady talked to 'em, mostly. I've no idea about his previous address." He looked at me slyly. "Woman chaser, wasn't he?"

"I don't know. Did he bring quite a few of them here?"

"Here——? The old lady would skin him alive. She don't miss anything."

"You really don't know much about him, then," I said.

"Nothing much. We weren't his—kind of company, I guess you'd say."

"What made you think he was a woman chaser, then?"

"Well, the way he dressed, I guess, and he was gone overnight quite a lot and he always smelled mighty good and the way the papers have been talking about that mystery woman supposed to have stabbed him——Well, a man can add two and two, I guess."

"Paid his rent on time?"

The old man nodded. "Good pay for nowadays." Suddenly, the old man sat more erectly in the chair, "Say, wait, there was a thing happened yesterday morning. Mr. Scott told me he was expecting a call and would I listen for it on his phone. He left his door unlocked, and I'm around here most of the time, anyway. He said he was expecting a call from a woman and to tell her the woman's friend was all right, that there wasn't anything to worry about. He said this woman who phoned might be nervous, but to be sure and tell her there was nothing to worry about, that somebody named Juan or something like that, he didn't frighten either one of them."

"And did the woman phone and did you give her that message?"

"I sure did."

"What was the woman's name?"

The old man closed his eyes. "Let's see now—it'll come, just a second now. Right pretty name. Ah—Sue Ellen, that was it. She didn't give a last name."

There was nothing further he could tell me; I thanked him, and left. Back on Sunset, I headed west.

Roger Scott and Rosa made a strange combination, but beds make strange bedfellows. And, of course, I had never met Roger and had yet to meet Rosa. People are not always as their friends and enemies see them.

Glenys Christopher had come to me because she'd seen my name in the paper connected with the Scott kill. That hand-wringing bit of corn about Bobby's adulation was only a bit designed to get me emotionally involved on their side.

I could be representing parties of diverse interests in the same case, and collecting from both of them. I could lose my license. I could even conceivably lose some front teeth if Pascal and Caroline caught me sticking my bent nose into a murder case.

On Doheny, I cut down to Santa Monica Boulevard and rode that all the way to Santa Monica. I cut over to Wilshire, then, and had lunch at Bess Eiler's new place.

And from there back to Venice and Windward Avenue, and the man behind the bar told me Sue Ellen wasn't around, but she was due.

I ordered a bottle of Eastern beer and put a couple of dimes into the juke box. At the end of the bar, a Mexican was reading the *Racing Form*. At a corner table, a wino dozed, his head cradled in his arms atop the table.

It was dim in the place and voices and traffic noises from outside seem to come from another world. From the juke box came Fats Waller's *Honeysuckle Rose,* played by the composer.

The bartender said, "He's dead, ain't he?"

I looked up, startled. "Who?"

"Fats Waller."

"Oh—Oh, yes—for some time. Yes, he's dead."

The bartender poured himself a short beer. "Couple guys had an argument about it in here the other night. Had to bounce one of them, finally."

I smiled at him. "You're big enough to do it. On this street, the bartenders have to be big or armed, don't they?"

He shrugged. "A drunk is a drunk on any street. They bounce a lot of them up there on The Strip, too, you notice. I go two-twenty."

I sipped my beer. Fats finished and Ellington came on.

The bartender said, "You're no midget, yourself. Don't I know you from somewhere? You wrestle or fight?"

I shook my head. "I played some guard for the Rams."

He stared at me suddenly. "The Rock—That's who you are. Brock the Rock—Brock Callahan, that's who you are."

I nodded modestly.

"What happened last year?" he asked. "Them lousy Forty-niners." He shook his head. "We knock off the champs twice, but can't lick the Forty-niners. It looked fishy to me."

"It wasn't," I said, and reached for a pretzel.

The door opened and a couple of young fellows came in. Both of them were wearing T shirts and blue jeans. Both of them were swarthy, husky and arrogant looking.

They both ordered rum and Coke.

The bartender looked at them disdainfully. "Cut it out, boys. We'd lose our license for sure. Neither one of you are old enough."

Both of them reached into their hip pockets. It was like a dancing team, almost. Two worn, Western-style wallets came out and were flopped onto the bar.

"Read 'em and weep, Pops," one of the boys said.

The bartender shook his head. "I've seen stolen driver's licenses before. So long, boys."

Silence for a moment, and then one of them said, "You

refuse to serve us? Maybe it's because you don't like Spanish-Americans, huh?"

The bartender looked at them levelly. "Nothing like that, boys, and you know it."

From the end of the bar, the Mexican who'd been reading the *Racing Form* spoke in soft Spanish, his eyes moving from one lad to the other as he talked.

The bartender came over to stand in front of me. "Hot-rod hoodlums," he said quietly. "Trouble, trouble, trouble, trouble—"

The man with the *Racing Form* had finished talking. The juke box had finished playing. The silence for a moment was almost absolute. From the table where the wino dozed came the sound of heavy breathing.

Then one of the boys said, "Okay, okay—make it straight Coke. We can have that, can't we, Pops?"

"Any time, boys." He put two glasses on the bar half-filled with cracked ice. He put a pair of bottles next to them.

The boys ignored the glasses. They took the bottles and went over to stand in front of the juke box.

I ordered another bottle of beer. The bartender shook his head and expelled his breath noisily. The wino dozed and the man at the end of the bar was making notes in a notebook, now. From the juke box came Stan Kenton.

The door opened again, and Sue Ellen came in. Her eyes went from the wino to the young men to me, to the wino again and back to me.

I said, "I've been waiting for you."

"How romantic," she said, and went past me to a doorway at the rear of the room. The door slammed behind her.

The bartender grinned and shook his head. "Ball of fire, ain't she? I'll put in a word for you." He went over to the closed door and through it, leaving it open behind him.

I looked over to find one of the blue-jeaners staring at me steadily. I returned the stare, a game I hadn't played since seventh grade. Ten seconds of that can make a man feel extremely adolescent but the kid wouldn't look away.

Then I felt a tap on my shoulder, and turned to see the bartender standing next to me. "She'll see you. I'll show you the room."

I followed him down a hallway past two washrooms to an open doorway near the end of the hall. It was a dressing room.

Sue Ellen said, "There's no place to sit, but I suppose you won't be staying long."

She sat on a bench in front of a dressing table. The bartender went back down the hallway.

There were photographs around the mirror of the dressing table, and one of the photographs was of Rosa. There was a curtained area that probably served as a closet and there was an odor of stale sweat and talcum powder in the small room.

I said, "You knew Roger Scott, didn't you?"

She shook her head. "I met him once, that's all. He was with Rosa, and I met him."

"Where's Rosa now?" I asked.

"I don't know."

"The police are looking for her in connection with a murder. You'd be smart to tell everything you know about Rosa, Sue Ellen."

"You're not the police."

"I know. And I haven't told them about you, as I should have. I will, now." I turned to go.

"Wait—" she said.

I turned back and waited.

"What's your beef with me, big boy? What'd I ever do to you?"

"Nothing," I said. "Neither to me nor for me."

"I owe you something? Why should I do anything for you?"

I didn't answer. I turned to go, again.

And again she said, "Wait—" And this time she added, "Damn you! Who the hell do you think you are?"

"Just a guy looking for Rosa Carmona," I answered wearily. "I'm getting paid to find her. She means nothing to me beyond that. I learned this morning that you phoned Roger Scott yesterday and were given a message by his landlord. The message concerned Rosa. I am looking for Rosa so I came back to you. And you tell me you don't know where she is, so I'm leaving. It's all very simple, isn't it?"

"Simple enough. But you have to put in a crack about calling copper. What was that for, sound effects?"

I said nothing.

She ran a hand into her bleached hair, removing a hair pin. She leaned forward and pulled off her shoes. She reached over for her purse on the dressing table.

I asked, "Nothing more to say?"

"Rosa's a friend of mine. But the only one who knew where she was after she left her apartment was this Scott guy. All messages went through him. Rosa was afraid that if I knew where she was staying, Mira would scare it out of me. So help me, God, I don't know where she is now. But I'm damned scared."

"You don't think *anybody* knows where she is now?"

"Whoever killed Scott might know."

"You don't think Rosa killed him?"

The blonde stared at me. "Gawd—no! Rosa kill somebody? Man, you're way off base. Rosa is soft as dough. Regular little love bug, not a mean bone in her body."

"Leading the life she led? She led a hard life."

"Hard—? Not if you like it, it isn't hard. Hell, she didn't need to hate any man. Rosa had all the men she wanted."

"Who killed Scott, then? And why is Rosa hiding?"

Sue Ellen shook her head. "I'm no cop, mister. I've told you all I know about it, every bit of it."

"Okay, Sue Ellen," I said. "Thanks a lot."

"Sure," she said. "Drop back when you're not playing Sam Spade. We'll hoist a couple."

"I might at that," I said, and waved and winked.

The blue jean boys weren't in the bar now, just the wino and horse player and the bartender. I nodded good-by to him and went out to where my flivver was waiting in the sun.

My flivver is what is known as the Victoria model and it has really deluxe upholstery in white and green plastic. Tufted and buttoned and with beaded edges, I was so proud of it.

I opened the door and turned sick.

Somebody had really worked the upholstery over with a knife. It was slashed viciously, both the front and rear seats. It was ruined.

CHAPTER FOUR

I WAS STILL standing in the street, the door on the driver's side open, when a man in a car parked against the opposite curb came out from his car and over to mine.

He said, "I saw those kids open the door and they looked kind of fishy to me. They had a rod parked right next to it, and I took their license number." He handed me a slip of paper.

"Thank *you*," I said. "Could I have your name, sir?"

The man smiled. "Look, mister, I *live* in Venice. My kids go to Venice High School. I don't want to tangle with those hot-rod hoodlums, and I don't want my kids to."

I didn't argue with him. I'd really been lucky to get as much as I had. I thanked him again for the number.

At the Venice Station, I showed them the upholstery and told them about the kids in the barroom and left the license number with them. Then I drove over to the West Side Station, on Purdue Street.

Trask was at his desk, and his smile wasn't too cool.

I told him about my day, right up to the slashed upholstery and the trip to the Venice Station. He leaned back in his chair, taking it all in with no great show of interest.

When I'd finished, he made a production out of taking a cigarette from a package, examining it, tapping it and lighting it.

"Take it over from where you picked up the package," I said. "There wasn't any film in the camera."

He smiled. "Brock, what did I tell you yesterday?"

"To keep my nose clean."

44

"That's right. And now, because you didn't, you have a carfull of slashed upholstery."

"And you might have something you didn't know, too. Right?"

He shook his head. "Wrong. Everything you told me, I already knew. And Sergeant Pascal knows more than I do about the case. How do you figure you're equipped to learn things we can't?"

"I don't know. I don't see how an extra man on the case is going to hurt any, though. Don't you want me to make a living, too?"

He studied the end of his cigarette.

"Not if you're working for a client who's interested in saving his sweetheart's neck. You don't think Mira would give her to us if he knew where she was, do you?"

"I suppose not. But I would. Remember, Lieutenant, I'm a citizen. That's always first with me."

"From where you sit now, maybe. But you're in a dirty business, Brock, and you can't stay clean in it, not if you want any new clients."

"That's cynical," I said. "The Department's in a dirty business, too."

"But we get paid by the people," he reminded me. "By all the people, not special interests, not people who have reasons to keep their troubles to themselves."

"There are going to be private investigators," I said. "I thought my reputation would make me one you'd be glad to see in the field. I guess I was wrong on that." I stood up.

He raised a hand. "Easy now, Brock. Don't go off half-cocked."

"I'm not, Dave. I can only take so much of this God-damned ham, though. You sit there like Ralph Bellamy in a cops and robbers movie, giving out with a Rotary luncheon speech. I don't have to listen to that, I hope."

He didn't look at his cigarette this time and he didn't smile. He said, "So long, Brock. And stay out from underfoot. Because we'll step on you hard."

"I've been stepped on by bigger men," I told him, "and better."

I thought that was a pretty good tag line and I left him on it.

At the Beverly Hills Ford Agency, I was told that they could get new seats and backs from Long Beach. They would order them.

At my office, I made out an insurance claim and then went to work on the reports of my calls for the day. Between Dave Trask's insolence and the hot-rodders' savagery, it hadn't been a pleasant day, but I was learning this wasn't a pleasant business.

Somewhere in the limbo between the law and the lawless I sat, respected by neither. My friends in the Department had been friends *before* I'd opened this office.

It was almost seven when the reports were finished. I phoned the Christopher residence and a maid answered and I asked to speak with Miss Christopher.

I told her what I'd learned and explained, "You must know some of his other friends. You could give me their names and I could talk to them. I've checked through the credit bureau and with his partner and his landlord. Without any other names to go on, I've done about as much as I can."

"You haven't learned who killed him."

"No, I haven't. And frankly, I have very little chance of learning it. I could take your money and pretend to spend my time on it. But that would be dishonest."

Silence, for a moment, and then she said, "Are you busy, now? Could you come to the house?"

"I haven't eaten," I told her. "Could you give me an hour for that first?"

"Eat here," she suggested. "I haven't eaten either. It's cool out here on the patio."

"I'm on the way," I said.

She wasn't wearing the suit this evening. She wore a white, bare-shouldered creation of some stiff, ribbed cotton, tight at the waist and with a flaring skirt.

There was a breeze from the west, but the night was warm. At a mammoth, brick grill, a Negro was broiling steaks.

Glenys Christopher asked, "Martini?"

"Only to keep a wealthy client. I'd prefer beer."

She smiled. "You can overwork this poor but honest motif, you know. Would you *really* prefer beer?"

"It's all I drink, usually."

From a refrigerated chest built into the planter that encircled the patio, she brought a bottle of Einlicher. It was a pilsener with a tang and no bars served it.

"The good life," I said, and leaned back in the cushioned redwood chair.

She sat across from me in the chair's twin. She said quietly, "I've been thinking of you all day."

A remark like that can be misread. I waited without comment.

"We need a man," she went on, "Bobby and I. We need a man I can trust and Bobby can admire. I'd like to put you on a retainer."

"Your parents are both dead?"

She nodded. "And there are no uncles or aunts with sense."

"You need an attorney," I told her. "Not a cheap peeper."

"We have an attorney, bright and completely ethical. Unfortunately, he isn't very muscular."

"Oh?" I sipped the beer. "You want a muscular man you can trust and Bobby can admire. Why—?"

"Because there are times when a displayed biceps is more effective than a letter from an attorney."

"You've had need lately for a strong man, have you?"

She sighed. "Not this month. You certainly don't encourage a customer who wants to buy, do you, Mr. Callahan?"

"I'm sorry," I told her. "Let's talk business after dinner. I'll bet I'll be more reasonable. It's been a messy day." I told her about the hot-rodders and my upholstery.

She was silent for seconds after I'd finished. Then she said, "And there, but for the grace of God, goes Bobby. He could be one of those. He's big and strong and there are times when he's arrogant. Don't you see why I need a man like you on call?"

I asked quietly, "Was Roger Scott that kind of man?"

Her answer was equally soft. "I thought he was. If what you learned today is true, I must have been wrong about him." She looked over at the grill. "I guess our steaks are ready."

Einlicher and filet, hot rolls and an all-green salad with imported Roquefort dressing. A warm night and a beautiful girl and Callahan offered a retainer. Why should I be uneasy?

An old Beverly Hills family, the Christophers. They had friends with money and the friends would have troubles and my office was convenient for all the troubled friends. Do not be naive, Brock Callahan; this is the world. It's a little more complicated than tackling a halfback or protecting a passer, but you've been offered a promising start in this new profession of yours.

The Negro asked, "Could I get you anything, Mr. Callahan?"

"You could bring me another bottle of that Einlicher," I told him.

I thought of Juan Mira and the three hundred dollars. I heard him say, "You find my Rosa—"

But I couldn't make a living on the Filipino trade. There weren't enough of them with money.

Glenys Christopher said, "You don't smoke and you drink only beer. You're a highly moral man, aren't you, Mr. Callahan?"

"I don't think so. I guess I just never got started on the pleasanter vices."

She chuckled. "On *any* of them?"

I looked at her directly. "I'm not a virgin, if that's what you mean, Miss Christopher."

She colored. "I guess that's what I meant, but your answer seemed unnecessarily vulgar."

"Blunt," I admitted, "but not vulgar. There seems to be a lack of frankness between us. Or am I only imagining things?"

No answer from her immediately. She ran a hand over the white dress, smoothing the wrinkles from her lap. She picked at an unseen bit of lint.

When she looked up again, she said, "Well, I guess it's not only Bobby I'm worried about. I need protection, too."

"From whom? From fortune hunters?"

"Mostly from myself, I guess. I thought that Roger was a talented writer and an ethical agent. He wasn't either of those things, was he?"

"I don't know. You could probably get informed opinions on both sides. Did he claim to be?"

She sighed. "Roger never directly claimed to be anything. He was a master at the modestly mentioned inference. He was far too intelligent to put himself out on any limbs."

"You've fallen out of love very quickly, Miss Christopher."

Her face stiffened. "With cause, I'm sure you'll agree?" I didn't answer. I didn't think a real love would end this quickly for any cause. It seemed like no one was going to mourn Roger Scott, neither his partner nor his girl nor his landlord.

I asked her, "Did Scott have any relatives you knew of?"

She shook her head.

"I'll have to see who's in charge of the funeral," I said. "There might be a lead there. Do you still think his enemies could be yours?"

She nodded.

I stood up. "It's been a tiring day, Miss Christopher. I see no reason for not accepting your retainer. And thank you for the wonderful dinner."

She rose. "You're welcome. And you could call me Glenys."

"All right. Good night, Glenys."

For a moment we stood there, immovable, and I had an urge to move closer, but she hadn't given my any reason for that. It was an urge any red-blooded boy would have. There were no servants in the patio, now; there was no sound but the rustling of the eucalyptus trees in the breeze from the west.

"Good night, Brock," she said finally. "Good luck."

I smiled. "You sounded just like Edward R. Murrow, there. If anything happens that I sould know about, let me know immediately, won't you?"

"I certainly shall. Wait, I'll walk with you to the door."

A gesture which made me a guest instead of an employee. We went from the yellow-lighted patio through the darkened house to the lighted entry hall. A maid was here, and she opened the door.

"Good night, again," Glenys said, and I said it again, and went along the asphalt of the parking area to my mutilated flivver.

The motor was still warm; her hundred and thirty horses came to life and we went humming down the driveway and onto Crescent Drive. West on Wilshire, west to Westwood, which is home.

The apartment house I lived in was old and Spanish, built around a court. It was still early; a few of the tenants sat in the court, enjoying that California rarity, a warm night.

The Kimballs, who lived in the apartment next to mine, were sitting near the iron stairway. Polly Kimball called out, "We're looking for a fourth, Brock. It's too early for bed."

"Not for me," I said. "I *work* for a living."

Paul laughed. "I told you you should have stayed with the Rams. Now you're learning what honest labor is."

I waved at them and went up the steps to 220. A small bedroom, a small living room, a small kitchen and a breakfast nook. And a bathroom with stall shower. I was in the shower two minutes later.

Drying myself, five minutes after that, I saw me in the full-length mirror on the bathroom door. Brock the Rock was really a block, not at all in the mythical tradition of the wedge-shaped American athlete. My legs were heavy and I was heavy through the middle and beefy through the chest. The Ram's medico had told me I was built for nothing else in the world but to play professional football; I had the build of a man who can take punishment. He should know; in his own playing days, he'd been the best in the business with the Bears.

I had always dreamed of being tall and willowy as a youth. I had wound up tall and not willowy. I had dreamed of being quick and deft, an All-American end. I had wound up steady and ready, an All-American guard.

And I had tried to develop a mind to go with the body, not quick, not deft nor flashy, but steady and persistent. I had tried to pick up a few virtues to give the appearance of steadiness some substance in fact. Which might sound silly, but we are shaped by our bodies. The big man fights, the small man runs and attitudes are born of both acts.

Thoughts for all occasions by B. Callahan; why all the introspection? I asked myself.

I hadn't been faced by any moral problems tonight. I had been offered a retainer by a wealthy client and had accepted the offer. I had tried to find Juan's Rosa without success, but the hunt was not over. Tomorrow was another day.

Tomorrow dawned muggy and hot with a low overcast. The *Times* had nothing new on the death of Roger Scott except for the information that a girl named Rosa Carmona was being sought by the police.

The Giants were five and a half games in front of Brooklyn. And in the American League, Cleveland was four games out in front of the Yanks. The Hollywood Stars were leading the Coast League. Cal's sensational freshman quarterback was transferring to UCLA, losing a year of eligibility in the process.

At Gilmore Field, Martinez had thoroughly whipped our local Art Arragon. Arragon's face looked like it had been worked over with a grater, but Golden Boy was eager for a rematch.

I had a couple of eggs and some bacon and four slices of raisin bread toast, all prepared by my dainty hands. I had two big glasses of milk and a cup of instant coffee.

I wondered what the police had learned, if there had

been any significant fingerprints in that motel room, if
they had any idea where Rosa was. Trask had made it
clear that any information I might get from the police, I
would have to get by reading the newspapers.

Of course, there was still Captain Apoyan at the West
Side Station, but it might be wise to save him for a time
when I really needed a friend. And maybe, with a client
like Glenys Christopher, I would command a little more
respect from the Department. It wouldn't figure that Juan
Mira would impress them.

And then, when I came across from the parking lot to
my office, I saw that the Callahan-Department relationship
was entering a new era. For Pascal and Caroline were
waiting in a Department car in front of my office building.

And they were both smiling.

Pascal got out on the curb side and his bloodhound's
face was genial. "Lieutenant Trask was a little short with
you, yesterday, I understand."

"That's understating it. Did he send you two over to
apologize?"

Pascal shrugged. "Well, let's say he realizes he was less
friendly than he could have been. And you did tell him
some things we didn't know, though he wouldn't admit it
yesterday."

"That bit about Sue Ellen phoning Scott's apartment?"
I guessed.

Sergeant Pascal nodded. "Who's this Sue Ellen?"

"She's the Savannah Songbird," I told him. "You boys
music lovers?"

Pascal chuckled. Behind the wheel, Caroline managed a
strained smile.

Pascal said genially, "Most private ops, I wouldn't give
you a plugged nickel for. But we're going to get along,
aren't we, Callahan?"

"Until you find out who Sue Ellen is," I admitted, "I

guess we are. Come on up; I've complete reports of all my activities upstairs."

Caroline came out from behind the wheel and both of them came up the stairs with me. In my office, I handed them the file copies of my two days of work.

Pascal had his notebook out and he must have found some things of interest, for he kept his pencil busy.

When he was finished, he said, "You don't know this Sue Ellen's last name?"

I shook my head. "But they can give it to you at that bar. Her picture is in the window, there."

Pascal nodded. He looked at Caroline and then back at me. "As long as you make one carbon of these reports, why not make two and send one to us as long as you stay on this Carmona disappearance?"

"And what do I get from you in return?"

"Look, Callahan *we're* the law."

"Not in Beverly Hills," I reminded him. "Isn't there anything you know about Rosa Carmona that I don't?"

Caroline lighted a cigarette, saying nothing, looking blank. Pascal frowned. "Well, we know she was mixed up with a hoodlum named Red Nystrom, one of Bugsy's old boys. But we haven't found him, though we know he's in town."

"And Roger Scott?" I asked. "Who's arranging for his funeral? Hasn't he any family?"

"I guess not. That partner of his, that Kramer, is taking the body. Funeral's this afternoon, if I remember right, at Elysian Fields."

"You've really nothing on Scott, at all, then?"

Pascal shook his head. "Hollywood type. God knows where they're spawned, but they don't seem to have any relatives or friends. At least, none that'll admit it." He folded his notebook and put it away. "Well, we'll go and shake down this Savannah Songbird. And find out, too, if there wasn't something else that old geezer at the apartment house forgot to tell us. We kind of overlooked him, because his wife did all the talking."

At the doorway, he said, "Keep in touch with us, Callahan. Keep us informed." The smile he'd brought with him was faded and gone.

"Yes, Sergeant," I said.

Rosa had originally intended to get away only from Juan. It seemed plain now that she was also trying to escape the law. Because if she was within reach of a newspaper or a news report, she would know the police wanted her.

I wondered if perhaps I could learn something at the motel the police hadn't learned. I'd been lucky with Scott's landlord. Perhaps my luck would hold.

I didn't learn anything the police didn't know. What I learned was what the police hadn't told me.

The manager of the motel was a man named Randall and I told him I was representing a friend of Roger Scott's and that the police hadn't been too cooperative. I'd remembered that Pascal had told Trask he was going to put the heat to this man.

Evidently Pascal had, for Randall was an irate citizen and eager to tell the world about it.

"—threatened me, too, the slobs," he told me. "Asked me what kind of a hot-pillow dive I was running. They've got no proof there was a girl in that room, but it's a girl they're looking for, according to the papers. Gives my place a fine reputation, doesn't it? Nothing in the paper about that Red Nystrom, is there? Maybe those brave bulls are scared of him, eh?"

"Red Nystrom—?" I asked. "What about him? Who is he?"

A hoodlum who used to work for the Syndicate, and now he's out on his own. A muscle-man. He was here, the day before, and he was threatening Scott. I heard him, and I told the law that. But they've got to give the papers the business about the *girl*, of course."

"That wasn't very nice," I agreed. "It does give you a bad rep." *And scares away the rest of that kind of trade,* I thought but didn't say.

"Even if I knew there was a girl there," he fumed, "what could I do about it? How many couples take their marriage certificates on trips with them?"

"Right," I said. "You're no mind reader. Anything else you could tell me about Roger Scott?"

"Well, let's see—" We were in his office, and he stared past me, through the window.

It was a thoughtful stare, at first. At least, that was my impression. But it grew to a frightened stare, and he said hoarsely, "Here he comes, now. He's just getting out of his car. Those stinking cops probably told him I—"

"Who's coming?" I asked.

"Nystrom, Red Nystrom." The voice was a whisper.

I turned to look out the window but I was too late. All I saw was the shoulder of a blue flannel jacket. It looked like a big shoulder.

And then the door slammed open, and I saw both shoulders. They were immense. Above them was a face that had been hit, in its day, but I could guess the face's owner had hit back. Above the face was a ring of red and curly hair around a tanned bald middle. The legs were what surprised me—pipe stems.

In that moment of his first appearance, I thought of pictures I'd seen of Bob Fitzimmons, Ruby Bob. This was that kind of build, all arms and shoulders.

The blue eyes in that lumpy face went from Randall to me and back to Randall. Nystrom nodded toward me. "Who's your friend?"

Randall didn't answer.

Nystrom said, "Tell him to blow; I want to talk to you."

Randall seemed almost petrified with fright. He looked nervously at me and licked his lips. He opened his mouth, and closed it.

I asked, "Is this Red Nystrom?"

Randall sort of half nodded, and Nystrom gave his attention to me. "Who are you, mister? And what's it to you who I am?"

"Take it easy," I told him. "I built my rep on bums like you, Red."

"Rep—? You a fighter, Laddie?"

I shook my head. "I'm a killer, Red. Killer Callahan from Beverly Hills."

Something approaching cognizance came to the battered face, and then he grinned. "Oh, that peeper—Yeh, I heard about you. Footballer, huh? Tough guy. Run along, footballer; my temper ain't so good, today."

I stood up and saw him measure me with his eyes. I said easily, "Put me out, Red. You're man enough, aren't you?"

His smile was anticipatory. "Sure, Laddie. Sure, I am." He took a step toward me, feet well apart.

"Gentlemen—please—!" Randal said chockingly.

Red took another step, and I waited. He was fairly close, now, but not close enough to swing—I thought, I'd overlooked the ridiculous length of his arms.

His open right hand came from nowhere and caught me smashingly on the left ear. I staggered sideways, and he came in, his head down.

I am no pugilist, but I know what to do when a man comes into me with his head down. I laced my fingers and brought both hands down on the back of his neck.

The same time that I pulled his head ever lower, I brought my knee up into the middle of his face.

That would have stopped a lesser man, right there. But Red only grunted and reached out to wrap his arms around my legs. I chopped down savagely behind his ear, but he kept coming, crowding me into the rear wall of the narrow office.

When you give a man your best, and he keeps coming, it is time to look for the nearest exit. I didn't have any; I was jammed into the corner, now.

And then, in that lost moment, I saw Randall go through a change of character and it gladdened my heart. Randall was picking up his chair, and it was a good, solid chair of Eastern maple.

He came up behind Red and lifted the chair high—and hesitated.

His eyes found mine, as though seeking approbation. His face was white and scared. Hitting a man with a chair is hard to do, the first time.

"He'll kill us both," I shouted. "Give it to him."

For a beginner, Randall did a first-rate job. He swung deeply, trying to catch Red's semibald noggin with the edge of the chair seat.

This put the legs of the chair close to my face on the way down, but I could see it coming, and Red couldn't. I pulled away in time and heard the satisfying "thunk" of the heaviest part of the chair connecting with Red's skull.

He grunted, and went down, and Randall grew drunk with power. Randall hit him again before I could get the chair away from him.

And then the door behind us opened, and a voice of authority said, "Hold it, right there!"

We turned to face Sergeant Pascal. He had his gun in his hand.

CHAPTER FIVE

"You can put the gun away, Sergeant," I said. "I think he's unconscious."

"What the hell is going on?" Pascal looked from Red to me and then to Randall. "Why the roughhouse?"

"That's Red Nystrom on the floor," I said. "You're looking for him, aren't you?"

"Never mind about that," he said. "I asked you a question."

Through the screen door, now, I could see Caroline, and Caroline had his gun out, too.

I said calmly, "Nystrom came barging in here while I was talking to Mr. Randall. He told me to beat it, but I hadn't finished talking and wasn't ready to leave. Red tried to throw me out."

Pascal's smile was thin. "And you—resisted. Is that what you're trying to tell me?"

I nodded. "Exactly. I hope it isn't illegal."

"Don't get smart, Callahan."

On the floor, Nystrom moaned.

I said, "Look, Sergeant, I'm not getting smart. But a business man in your district has been threatened by a hoodlum. He not only resisted; he probably saved me from a serious beating by that hoodlum. You're a little confused, I think, Sergeant. *The hoodlum is the one on the floor.*"

"Don't raise your voice, Callahan. My hearing's okay."

"Yes, but your brains are scrambled," I said. "I was trying to get through to them."

Pascal studied me quietly and ominously. Caroline came through the doorway, and the screen door slammed behind him. On the floor, Nystrom stirred.

I still had the chair I'd taken away from Randall. I set it down in a corner.

Randall said, "I hit Nystrom with the chair. I would have hit him some more, if Mr. Callahan hadn't taken the chair away from me. I would have killed him, I bet. The police protection a man gets in this town, we have to—"

He'd been wound up, and now he suddenly unwound. He looked at the blood seeping out of Red's bald crown and turned blindly toward the doorway, seeking air.

Caroline stood in front of the door, his short, fat figure effectively blocking it.

I said sharply, "Out of the way, Fatso; the man's sick."

Caroline didn't move. He glared at me.

Then Randall put a hand to his mouth and retching sounds came from within him, and Caroline moved quickly to one side. Randall staggered out and in a moment the sound of his retching came back to us.

I said quietly, "Don't you think someone better phone for an ambulance? Nystrom could have a concussion, you know."

Nystrom might have heard and wanted to prove his toughness. In any event, he moaned again and put a hand under his chest to push himself up. He was on his knees and hands as Pascal put his gun away and came over to help him up.

Pascal said, "Need a doctor, Nystrom?" and the red head shook stubbornly.

Nystrom, with Pascal's help, got to his feet, his back to Caroline and me. When he turned, I saw what my knee had done to his face. His nose was flattened and bleeding, one eye was already puffed and turning blue.

"We'll meet again," he said to me. "Don't forget that, Callahan."

I nodded. "I guess we will, Red. Next time, I'll have a gun."

He nodded. He meant he'd have a gun, too, but it wasn't something he'd voice in front of the law.

Pascal said, "Put your hands behind you, Red." He took his cuffs out.

Nystrom's voice was rough. "What's the charge? A couple of mugs work me over with a chair, and *I* get the cuffs. How about *them*?"

"They're going along," Pascal said quietly. "We'll teach the three of you a little respect for the law, down at the station."

Red and Randall rode in back with Pascal; I rode in front with Caroline. The Department car was hot and Caroline's B.O. was heavy on the muggy air. I opened one of the wings to divert a breeze into the car.

Down at the station, Randall and I were separated from Red. Red went to a cell; Randall and I went into Lieutenant Trask's office.

Pascal came with us and Caroline stayed with Red. Pascal hadn't said a word to me since I'd made the remark about his scrambled brains.

I heard that remark repeated along with the others as Pascal gave Trask the story of it. Just as Pascal finished, a reporter stuck his head through the doorway.

"Secret session, Lieutenant?" the reporter asked, and Dave Trask nodded.

"C'mon, Lieutenant," the reporter persisted. "It can't be that important."

Trask looked at him bleakly. "Later, Braham. Wait in the hall. And close that door."

The door closed and Trask looked at me. "Well, Callahan?"

I gave it all to him, just at it had happened.

Trask looked at Pascal. "Nystrom have a gun on him?"

Pascal shook his head.

Trask looked back at me. "What were you doing over at that motel?"

"Talking to Mr. Randall."

"About what."

I braced myself. "I was soliciting his business."

Randall muttered something and Trask looked at him sharply. "What was that?"

Randall didn't look at him.

"Don't be afraid to speak up, Mr. Randall," I said. "Don't forget they're working for us. We're paying their salaries."

Pascal said sullenly, "Maybe Callahan needs time to cool off, Lieutenant? Maybe he needs a place to think things over?"

Trask didn't answer. I said, "Did you get anything out of that lead I gave you this morning? Did you learn anything from Sue Ellen?"

Neither of them said a word.

I said harshly, "Damn it, I've cooperated all the way. And get this hoodlum treatment."

Trask waved a hand. "Slow down, Brock. Take it easy. You've a tendency to be insolent."

"If I am, I apologize. But don't forget my dad was a cop and he was killed by a hoodlum. You know what side of the fence I'm on, Dave."

Trask nodded and said, "I remember and I think I know what side of the fence you're on. I guess we could all watch our tongues a little." He looked at Pascal.

Pascal muttered something that could have been apology.

Trask looked back at me. "I guess we won't need a statement from you two. To tell the truth, I'm not sure we want Red locked up. We've been watching him, Brock. Pascal and Caroline followed him to that motel."

I said nothing. I stood up.

Randall stood up and asked, "Do we get a ride back to the motel?"

"You'll get a ride," Pascal said. "I'll take you."

Randall and I rode in the back, Pascal and Caroline in the front. It was a quiet trip; nobody said one word. They dropped us off at the curb in front and drove away without even nodding good-by.

"Cops—" Randall said, and shook his head.

"They're underpaid," I told him, "and overworked. They deal with rapists and murderers, with child-molesters and wife-beaters. All day long they meet arrogance and deceit and hate. You can't expect they'd have the same attitude as ministers."

Randall didn't comment on that. What he said was, "That Nystrom will be back, I bet. I'd better clean up that old service .45 of mine."

"Sure," I said, "but take it easy. And thanks for your work with that chair. That took a lot of guts."

His smile was modest. "I surprised myself."

At the drugstore on Beverly Drive, the special was short ribs and browned potatoes. It was too hot for that; I ordered a bacon and tomato sandwich and a vanilla milk shake.

The counterman said, "This Odie Posey's back with the Rams, huh? He should go good, right?"

I nodded.

"I'll still take that Skeet Quinlan," he said. "Man, how that little guy can twist and turn, huh?"

"He's a sweetheart," I agreed. "Get the bacon lean, won't you? Get the fat cooked off."

He made an O with thumb and forefinger. "You bet I will, Brock. Nothing's too good for the Rock."

It is a discerning man who realizes the true worth of a lineman. This counterman deserved more than life was giving him.

My mail consisted of three ads and a throwaway weekly newspaper and a letter with a lump in it. The letter was addressed to "Juan Mira, c/o Brock Callahan." The lump felt like a ring.

The postmark was 6 A.M. this morning from Santa Monica.

I phoned Juan, but there was no answer. I put the letter into a more or less hidden compartment behind the bottom drawer in my desk.

Then I washed up in the washroom down the hall and drove out to Elysian Fields. On the drive out, I thought about my dialogue with Lieutenant Dave Trask. For the second time, Dave had given me the impression I'd told him nothing new, had helped not at all.

The first time, he had lied, and I wondered if he'd lied this last time. One thing I'd noticed, he'd made no request, this time, for me to keep my nose out of the case. Perhaps he had just overlooked it. Or perhaps not.

There would be a short service for Roger Scott in the rather impressive chapel at Elysian Fields. And it was just about to begin as I entered.

The chapel would seat over a hundred, but there was no need for that many seats this afternoon. I was one of the three in attendance.

Joe Kramer sat in the front row. Two rows back of him, there was a feminine head of brownish-blonde hair above a pair of blue gabardine shoulders. Neither of them looked around as I came in and took a seat in the back.

The minister did the best he could with what he had. He was supplied by the management and he'd had no personal knowledge of Roger Scott. He spoke of "the word that lingers when the man is gone" and "this untimely extinguishing of the creative spark." He sounded as though he were reading a speech written by someone else. Probably Joe Kramer, who now owned the business and could afford to be tolerant about the deceased.

Elysian Fields borders a golf course, and the hole they'd dug for Roger Scott was only about twenty yards from the fence that ran along the thirteenth fairway.

The pallbearers were professionals, but they waited at the grave with the three of us, to make it look less lonely.

And then, just as the minister began to drop his handful of dirt onto the coffin below, there was a shout of "Fore!" from the thirteenth tee.

Some dub had really sliced his drive. I was facing the tee; I saw the ball coming, and ducked.

The ball bounced twice—and rolled into the grave. I heard a hollow "thump" as it hit the coffin.

I straightened, shaken. The minister had paused for only a moment; he continued with the "dust to dust." Joe Kramer's face was a mask, as were the pallbearers'. The blonde was pale, and she was biting her lower lip.

She was an attractive girl, fairly short, nicely shaped, and her brown eyes were warm and large. She looked at me, and down at the grave. Her hands were folded tightly.

The last words were said, and everybody turned to go back the way we'd come. At the fence, I caught a wave from one of the golfers and I went over there.

"Did you see a ball come in here?" he asked.

He was a stocky man in a loud shirt and his wide face was bland and unconcerned.

"I hope you hit a provisional," I told him. "That slice of yours wound up in the wrong hole."

"No kidding? In the grave?"

"Mmmmm-hmmm. That's where it is."

"They haven't started to fill it up, yet, huh?"

I shook my head. "The diggers aren't around. But there's a question of good taste involved, don't you think?"

"Good taste, hell," he said. "That was a new ball."

He was climbing over the fence as I went down the road to join the others.

In the parking area, the brownish-blonde headed for a mustard-colored Chev Bel Air. I got to the car before she had finished closing the door.

I said, "My name is Callahan, M'am, and I've been hired to investigate this—thing that happened."

She looked at me with the warm brown eyes, but said nothing. She looked at me without much interest.

I said quietly, "I've so little to go on, I'm grasping at straws. I hope you don't think I'm being—pushy about this, but I could certainly use any information you might have about Roger Scott."

"I haven't any," she said. "I met him through Glenys Christopher. You're working for Miss Christopher, aren't you?"

I nodded.

"Well, she knows as much about him as I do. Good afternoon, Mr. Callahan."

The Chev came to life, and she swung it in a U-turn, heading for the street. Next to me, Joe Kramer said, "Nice dish. Those eyes could melt you, couldn't they?"

"Or burn you," I added. "It wasn't much of a funeral, was it, Joe? I'm surprised there weren't a few curiosity-seekers, at least."

"No notice in the papers," Joe said. "Well, I've got to

get back to work. I'm up to my ears in scripts." He sighed. "I sometimes wonder if there are people in the world who *don't* write."

Along the path that led to Scott's grave, the diggers were going to replace most of the earth they'd dug out this morning. On the thirteenth green, the foursome was putting. Overhead, a sky-writer was spelling out "Coola-Cola —It's Coola."

The Ford came to life and snorted in disgust. "Everybody dies," I told her. "Thousands every day. You can't expect the living to mourn them *all*."

The flivver didn't deign to answer me, murmuring to herself.

Through the overcast, the sun was now breaking through. I turned right on Sepulveda, heading for Sunset. It was still too early for the going-home traffic; I made good time all the way.

My phone-answering service told me I'd had a call, and the number was Mira's. I called him back.

I said, "There's a letter here for you in care of me. Want to drop over and pick it up?"

"I come right now," he said.

I had taken the license number of the Chev at Elysian Fields and I included it in my report of the day's work. I could ask Glenys who the girl was. If she didn't know, I could then check it through the license bureau.

And then I remembered, I had never really questioned Mr. Randall. Red had broken that up just as Randall could have been about to give me something. I phoned the motel.

When he answered, I told him, "You were about to tell me something, I think, when Nystrom broke up the party this morning. Can you remember what it was?"

"About this Roger Scott, was it?"

"I think so."

Silence, and then, "Well, I've forgotten it in all the excitement, I guess. If I think of anything, Mr. Callahan, I'll sure call you."

"Please do," I said.

I went back to work on the reports, and my phone rang. It was Glenys Christopher. "Do you swim, Mr. Callahan?"

"Not professionally, but I can get around in the water. Why?"

"Oh, I thought we'd have a few people in for a little party. And I think the night will be warm enough to use the pool. And I'd like you to come."

"Any special occasion?"

"Well—" Silence, and then, "I thought it might be appropriate. I didn't want anyone to think I was mourning. Do you understand?"

"No, but I'm not subtle. I went to the funeral."

"Oh—?" Silence.

"Just Callahan and Scott's business partner and a girl with a Chev Bel Air—those were the only mourners."

Silence.

I asked, "Are you still there?"

"I'm here. I can't think of anything to say, particularly."

"Do you know the girl with the Chev? She knows you. Pretty girl, very fine figure, brownish-blonde hair—"

"And a crooked eye tooth?" Glenys asked.

"I didn't notice. She wasn't smiling."

"I think I know the girl. She is an incurable sentimentalist. Are you coming to the party or not?"

"I'll be there. What time?"

"After dinner. Eight-thirty or nine."

"Thank you. Do you want to tell me the girl's name?"

"Not particularly. She's too available. I'll see you tonight." The line went dead.

I was finished with the reports and sitting by my window, watching the traffic, when Juan Mira came in.

He wore a fawn-colored suit, today, the jacket almost down to his knees. He wore a brown shirt and a white string tie and brown-and-white sport shoes with heavy crepe soles.

I fished the letter out of the compartment and handed it to him. He tore it open eagerly.

There was no letter inside, only a diamond ring, big and ornate. Juan stared at it dully.

"Is that the ring you gave her, Juan?"

He nodded. "No note? No nothing?"

"That's all I got, right there. Let me keep the envelope, though. Maybe the police can learn something from that."

"To hell with them," he said. "I don't want them in my business."

"They're already in up to their hips, Juan. They're looking for her, and her not showing up makes it worse for her every day. She's still the number-one suspect for Scott's death, you know."

"You find her," he said. "And you get me a good lawyer for her. To hell with the police." He took his wallet out. "More money?"

I shook my head. "No, no more money. All right, Juan, I'll keep working."

"That Sue Ellen, keep working on her. She knows, I bet."

Juan left and I took the envelope the ring had been in and put it into a larger envelope addressed to Lieutenant Dave Trask. I enclosed a note explaining everything.

It was a slow trip to Westwood in the jammed traffic of Wilshire. Stop and go, stop and go—another straw to add to the other straws of this day, frustration and futility.

What had I accomplished, what had I learned?

Nothing.

Being paid by two clients and serving neither one well. Why had I considered myself qualified to open that office? Playing cops and robbers is fun, but most of us outgrow it in the fourth grade. And if I really wanted to play cop, the Department was looking for men.

But who wanted to play cop at those prices?

In front of the Los Angeles Country Club, a mustard-colored Chev Bel Air went past me in the inner lane. I saw the dark blonde hair and tried to remember what the license number had been on the car at Elysian Fields.

The Chev turned right on Beverly Glen and I didn't follow. Glenys knew the girl and I still had the license number in the office.

Left on Westwood Boulevard and home. In my mailbox, there were two ads and a letter from my aunt in La Jolla. She wanted to know, as long as I wasn't playing football this year, why I didn't come down for a visit? There were so many interesting young people in La Jolla, I'd be guaranteed a good time.

Feminine young people, my aunt meant. To her, an unmarried man is a great waste.

A hot shower, and a cool one. Then I put on a pair of shorts and made my dinner, lamb chops and creamed potatoes and broccoli. And a bottle of Milwaukee beer to go with it, and I felt better. A Beverly Hills party in prospect, two satisfied clients, one who wanted me on a retainer basis; why had I been gloomy before dinner?

I had a fine imported linen suit I rarely wore because my legs are too heavy for fabrics that are not wrinkle resistant. But the evening would be cooler than the day and I would probably spend most of my time at the party in swimming trunks. I wore the suit with a white on white shirt and a Countess Mara tie my aunt had sent me for Christmas last year. I thought I looked pretty sharp.

CHAPTER SIX

THERE WERE a few cars already parked in the parking area at the side of the Christopher home when I tooled the flivver in at nine o'clock. One was a Jag and the other two were Cads. The flivver snorted before I turned her off.

I was just getting out when the mustard-colored Chev came rolling in. I waited until she'd parked.

She was in strapless black, this evening, with a white, crocheted stole over her shoulders. She looked at me curiously as she approached. The lights serving the parking area were yellow and dim.

I said, "As a fellow-driver of a lower income group car, I thought it might be fitting if we went in together."

"Perhaps we could use the servants' entrance," she said. "Brock Callahan, isn't it?"

"At your service. And you?"

"It doesn't matter, Mr. Callahan. I'm sure I'll never require your services."

"What are you, a Forty-niner fan, or something? What'd I ever do to you to earn this scorn, Miss—?"

She stopped walking and looked up at me. "I'm sorry. I really am. You're just one of the moths, really, aren't you, attracted by the flame?"

"I think I'm a little heavy to fly," I answered. "Who or what is the flame?"

"Glenys Christopher, of course. Who else?"

"You're here," I said. "Are you a moth?"

"I'm a butterfly," she said, "working by day and flitting by night. And meeting very few interesting people, except at parties given by Glenys Christopher."

"I see. And that's important to you, meeting interesting people?"

"That's important to me. And meeting *wealthy* people is not only important, it's necessary. I'm an interior decorator, Mr. Callahan."

"Oh," I said, "I get it. What name do you use in the trade?"

Silence, and then she chuckled. "Persistent, aren't you? My name is Jan Bonnet. That's middle-class enough, isn't it?"

"I can see the sign," I said, "reading 'Décor by Jan Bonnet.' My arm, Miss Bonnet?"

We went along the walk together to the open front door. A maid met us there, and then Glenys Christopher came out from the living room.

She frowned. "Did you two come together?"

"More or less," I said. "We met this afternoon."

Jan said, "He's trying to be humorous, Glen. We met in the parking area a few minutes ago."

A moment of silence while Glenys studied me. Then she smiled and said, "A few people are already here. I think you know them all, Jan. Les Hartley's here."

"Goodie," Jan said, without expression. "I'll manage." She left us and went into the living room, heading for the bar in one corner.

Glenys sighed. "I do admire her. But she seems to—*resent* me for some reason."

She took me into the living room and I met some people. I met them by name and not by occupation, so I didn't learn until later what Jan Bonnet had meant by 'interesting people.' Most anyone is interesting when he's talking about his specialty; these people had interesting specialties, I learned later.

There was a ceramist and a folk singer, a gag man and

a sculptor, a sports announcer and a wrestler. They were the early birds and still sober; the party was still in its strained and quiet-voiced birth.

Glenys left me to go and welcome some new people; I went over to the bar for a bottle of that Einlicher.

From the window here, I could see the pool, and it was a sixty footer, with both high and low boards. I took my glass and the bottle out there.

Jan Bonnet sat in a deck chair on the patio side of the pool, and Bobby Christopher sat next to her on a canvas and aluminum chair. I went over.

Bobby looked up and grinned. "Hi, Champ. I've made up my mind. S.C. for me."

"Great," I said, "especially if you want to build a rep."

He nodded. "That's what I want." He stood up. "Well, I've got to pick up my date. I'll be back."

I took the seat he'd vacated. I took a swig of the beer. Jan Bonnet sipped her drink; it looked like a Bloody Mary.

I said, "Having fun?"

"It's too early for that. Just the exhibits are in there, now. The audience arrives later."

"The audience would be Glenys' *real* friends?"

She nodded.

"Why do you resent her?" I asked.

"Because she feeds on people, more talented people, more truly important people. Her money attracts them and her parasitic ego finally kills them."

"You think Roger Scott was talented and important?"

"I certainly do."

"And handsome, too, wasn't he? A real lady-killer."

The brown eyes were neither soft nor warm. "That was cheap."

"I try to deal in the realities," I said. "He was a reading

fee agent and a vanity press author. He was apparently shacked up with a honky-tonk stripper when he died. For a woman in business, you certainly have a strange soap-opera outlook, Jan Bonnet."

Her voice was low. "You didn't even know him, did you?"

"Not when he was alive. How well did you know him?"

"I knew him very well."

"All right," I said. "I could be wrong. Is Glenys stifling your talent, too?"

Her voice was a monotone. "I don't think, Mr. Callahan, that you and I have anything to say to each other. Couldn't you find some other guest to annoy?"

"I'll try." I stood up. "If I've been rude, I'm sorry."

For a moment, I thought I saw a flicker of apology in the brown eyes. But she said nothing, and I went away from there.

I talked with the gag man, but he was out of gags. I talked with the sculptor, but it didn't take him long to realize my interest was more polite than informed. I talked with the sports announcer, but he was a Forty-niner partisan. The folk singer had big hips and no bust and a heavy mustache and very little party dialogue.

I got another bottle of Einlicher and was heading for a corner to sulk in, when Bobby came back with his date. She was only about eighteen, but she would never need any more than she had right now.

Bobby said, "C'mon, Brock, these people will bore you silly. We're getting up two teams for water polo."

In the men's dressing room, the freshly laundered trunks were stacked according to size, each in its own pliofilm wrapping. There were lockers along the wall with built-in coat hangers, and there were sun lamps set into the tile walls. The muscle-building equipment was in here, too, a rowing machine, bar bells, forearm developer.

Bobby's smile was wry. "From my Muscle-Beach days. What a freak I was turning into until I got smart."

"Muscle-bound?" I asked.

He nodded. "I looked like Mr. America. I couldn't catch a baseball or throw one. I couldn't run to the corner without falling over my own feet. It took a lot of tennis and swimming to make me look like a human being again."

"I never went down to Muscle-Beach," I said, "but I've seen the boys in the newsreels."

Bobby inclined his head toward the living room. "That would-be wrestler in there is one of them. Maybe he'll get into trunks later and you can see what I almost became."

I captained one team, and Bobby the other. We started with two people on a side and wound up with five. The wrestler joined my team about halfway through the game, and I saw what Bobby meant.

He was all bunched muscle and barrel-chest. His thighs were outsized hams and his stomach was a washboard. He was as agile as an elephant on stilts.

Half the players were feminine and he concentrated his contact work on them. He was a great man for the underwater caress.

A few of the girls withdrew from the game and a few of the husbands and boy friends began to mutter.

I said to Bobby, "We'd better break this up before there's a riot. Or one of us could drown the bum?"

"We'll break it up," Bobby said. "I'll concede the game, and Muscles won't have any beef."

Which he did.

I put on a terry cloth robe supplied by the management and retired to the pool's edge with a bottle of beer. The divers took over, the exhibitionists.

There was a full moon, and it was a warm night. This should have been fun, but I got to thinking of Roger Scott and Rosa Carmona.

On the high board, Glenys Christopher was poised. She had the most beautiful long legs I'd ever seen on a woman and unless her suit had built-in cheaters, she was properly endowed above the waist.

Her slim body arched in a full gainer and straightened in time for perfect, splash-less symmetry.

Jan Bonnet came along the pool-side marble in a Bikini suit, and the image of Glenys dimmed. Jan had one of those perfect, small figures. She was carrying another Bloody Mary.

She sat down next to me. "I want to apologize."

"Accepted. Have you a crooked eyetooth?"

"Uh-huh?" Her lips parted. "See?"

"Cute," I said. "It saves you from being perfect. Are we friends?"

"We're not enemies, I guess. Why?"

"I want to be friends with you. There aren't many interior decorators who can decorate the interior of a swimming suit like you can."

"Thank you. Who told you about the eyetooth, or did you notice it before?"

"Glenys Christopher told me about it. And she told me you were an incurable sentimentalist."

"That's not true. I'm in business. There are no sentimentalists in business in this town."

"Shall we go back to Roger Scott?"

She looked at me frankly. "Why? What's there to be said about him now? What's there to be gained by talking about him?"

"I've been hired to find his killer. You might know something that would help me do that."

She shook her head slowly. "I can't think of anything that would help. He gambled, some, I know. Do you think that perhaps some gambler might——?" She looked at me quizzically.

"Not fourteen times with a knife," I said. "Most gamblers I've met would play it cooler than that."

She looked down at her drink. "I suppose. Who is this—this Rosa person the police are looking for?"

"She's a singer. She's how I got into the case. Her fiancé hired me to find her."

"A—singer? Is she the—stripper you mentioned before?"

"That's right."

A pair of slim, tanned, wet legs came into my line of vision and I looked up to see Glenys smiling at me. "You two are being very exclusive, aren't you? I don't think Brock could afford a really expensive decorator, Jan."

"She wasn't selling me," I said. "I was trying to sell her."

"Oh?" Glenys didn't smile. "Yourself or your services?"

Jan got to her feet. "I'll mix. I can use the business." She went over to put her drink on a table. She took two quick steps and her fine body slanted down into a shallow, racing dive. She went the length of the pool in a lazy crawl.

Glenys dropped down beside me. "She has a fine figure for a small woman, hasn't she?"

I nodded, and swigged at my beer.

"I suppose she's been filling you up with a lot of misinformation about Roger."

I shook my head. "I tried to get her to talk about him, but she didn't want to."

At the other end of the pool, the wrestler had plopped into the water next to Jan.

"She adored him," Glenys said quietly. "She hated me when I was going with Roger. She's man-crazy."

"Not completely, the way it looks," I said.

Jan had just brought a right hand from right field and the wrestler had been on the receiving end. He reached for her as I stood up.

I said, "We don't want any unpleasantness at your party, do we?" I trotted down the near side of the pool.

Jan had gone under water, and the wrestler was still on top, about to dive under after her.

"Look out, below," I shouted in my jovial voice. And threw my scant two hundred and seven pounds onto his broad back.

He went down like a rock and came up gasping. Water was mixed with his curses and then he got one of those set, theatrical grins and he reached out for my arm.

I saw Jan climbing out of the pool, and I swam away from Muscles. He came churning after but I had twenty feet on him when I climbed out again at the end where Glenys still sat.

The water was only hip-high, here. Muscles stood in it, looking up at us. "That wasn't very funny, big boy. You could have broke my back."

I nodded. "I know. I considered that."

"Maybe you wanna fight, huh?"

"Without a rehearsal? Don't be silly, Muscles; Equity would take away your card."

Glenys said soothingly, "Let's not get riled, Duke. Brock didn't mean any harm, I'm sure. That girl is a particular friend of his."

"Okay," Duke said. "So that's different. Whyn't he just tell me, lay off? So, okay."

He went churning off toward the deep end again, agile as a pig with a broken back.

Glenys smiled. "You're big, but not big enough to fight professionals, are you?"

"Wrestlers are not professionals," I said. "Unless you mean professional actors, and they wouldn't qualify as that by theatrical standards."

"My, we're angry."

"Yes. I love all kinds of sports and in sports, *professional* means the top. I hate people who debase any sport, and that's what wrestlers have done."

"And made millions doing it."

I looked at her. "Does that make it all right?"

A voice from my other side said, "I guess it does, today."

I turned to see that Jan had sat down next to me. She was holding a big hamburger sandwich. She said, "Thank you for the rescue, Sir Launcelot. You do improve with knowing, don't you?"

Glenys said, "Well, I must circulate." She stood up and moved toward the living room.

Bobby's girl friend was on the high board and a lot of eyes were turned her way.

Jan asked, "Why do *young* and shapely girls attract more attention than older shapely girls?"

"From men?"

"Well—yes, from men."

"If used cars and new cars were the same price," I asked, "who'd buy a used car?"

The young body came hurtling down, the arms wide in a swan dive. At the deep end, Duke swam over toward where the girl had gone in.

"I think I'll get one of those hamburgers," I said. "Where are they handing them out?"

"Next to the bar. Hurry back, won't you?"

Too many Bloody Marys? The door-like contours of my

big body? My witty conversation? There had been a change in the attitude of Jan Bonnet.

I came back. And later, after we'd dressed again, I danced with her to the music of the big record player in the play room. I danced with Glenys, too, and Bobby's girl, who was named Dianne. I even danced with the folk singer, though she was harder to move than the Bear line. I'd had enough Einlicher by then; I would have danced with Duke if he could follow.

I kept coming back to Jan and she didn't seem to mind. And then people began to leave, and Jan said, "Well, tomorrow is a working day. It's been fun, Brock Callahan."

I nodded. "I hope I'll see you again."

"Professionally?"

I shook my head.

She smiled. "You probably will."

It was a remark I was to wonder about later, and not much later. Because she came back in a few minutes, and said her car wouldn't start, and did I know anything about cars?

"Not Chevs," I told her, "but I can take a look at it."

So I looked under the hood and saw nothing wrong and tried to start it with no success. So I suggested she leave it here, and I would take her home.

And I went in to pay my respects to my hostess and I told her about Jan's car.

Glenys' smile looked a little frigid to me. She made no comment, however.

In the parking area, the interior lights went on as I opened the door of my flivver.

Jan saw the slashed upholstery and said, "Migawd, what happened?"

I told her what had happened as we drove down to Sunset. Here, I turned right automatically.

"Hoodlums," she said. "The papers are full of them. Doesn't it frighten you?"

"A little."

"How did you know I lived this way?"

"I was going home, today, from the office and I saw you turn into Beverly Glen. Is that where you live, or were you taking it to the Valley?"

"No, I live in the Canyon. It was just *chance* that you saw me, Brock?"

"Of course. What else?"

"Nothing else. I'm sorry. I'm a—a—an old maid in a lot of ways, I guess."

I turned on the radio and got a platter program. The moonlight bright bends of Sunset unwound under the flivver's humming tires. Soft and sentimental music came from the speaker.

Jan asked softly, "What did Glenys say when you told her you were taking me home?"

"Nothing. Absolutely nothing."

"Mmmm-hmmm. This is a ridiculous town, isn't it?"

"How?"

"She hates me and I hate her. And she has a party and I come running. How phoney can people get?"

Nothing from me. The radio came through with a commercial, and I swung the flivver up Beverly Glen. There shouldn't be any reason for me to be a little short of breath; the Chev wouldn't start, and I was simply a means of transportation to the girl. I was wrong, I told myself, in putting a Duke connotation on it.

Jan said, "Turn left at the next side road."

I turned left and followed a narrower road up an incline to a small house on the right.

Jan said, "This is home. Could I interest you in one more bottle of beer?"

CHAPTER SEVEN

In the morning, I wakened to the sound of a dog barking and the smell of coffee. From the big bed, I could see the living room but not the kitchen. The coffee smell must come from the kitchen; I didn't know where the dog's bark was coming from.

We'd talked a little, last night, and she'd told me this was too small a house to do anything spectacular with. So she'd torn out a lot of walls, giving some impression of spaciousness and tried to make the place comfortable, if not impressive. It had an open feeling, each specialized area melted into the other without an effect of rooms, but also without an air of the one room, utility cabin effect.

The dog continued to bark and the coffee smell grew richer. I climbed out of bed and found a razor in the bathroom. The bathroom must be new; there was a really deluxe stall shower, tiled to the ceiling, and with a ribbed floor.

I shaved before my shower and saw the bruised cut on my lower lip. Her eyetooth must have been sharp as well as crooked.

When I came into the kitchen, she smiled. Then she saw the cut lip and looked away. I thought she blushed a little.

"Peaceful up here, isn't it?" I asked. "Except for that damned dog. Is it yours?"

"No. A neighbor's. I—Do—I—What the hell does one say in the morning?"

"Good morning. Are we having eggs?"

"If you want. Don't get any ideas, Brock Callahan. There are times when I simply—I mean, there's a definite therapeutical need for some form of release in a society as hectic as—"

"Relax, Jan," I said. "Don't beat it to death, honey."

She smiled. "I told you I was an old maid."

"You lied," I said. "Should I fix the eggs? I'm pretty good at it."

"All right. Sunnyside up for me."

The kitchen was a farm kitchen, beamed, and with one old brick wall into which the range was built. We ate in a windowed corner, and the *Times* was on the table.

The police, I saw at a glance, were still seeking Rosa Carmona and she was now identified as the fiancée of Juan Mira. There wasn't too much space given to the story.

Jan said, "You'd better not drive me back for my car. Glenys will see us and add two and two."

"Why don't you have a garage man pick it up, fix it, and deliver it here?" I suggested.

"That's an idea," she said.

I smiled. "Did you try to fix it, last night?"

She frowned, and shook her head.

I said, "I noticed some grease on your fingers, and I thought that maybe you—"

She was blushing fully now, and looking intently at the window to her left.

I said softly, "I am a beast. And there is a definite therapeutical need for some sort—"

"Shut up!" she said. Her brown eyes blazed at me.

"I should have checked the distributor rotor," I ploughed on. "Do you have it in your purse?"

"Please," she said hoarsely. "Would you leave?"

"No. Jan, honey, you're a sweet and honest girl and that's wonderful. You and I don't need to be phoney with each other. We're friends, remember?"

She was still blushing, but the eyes no longer blazed.

"All right, guilty. Couldn't we talk about something else?"

"I'd like to talk about Roger Scott," I told her, "but I've a feeling you don't. At any rate, you don't want to tell me much about him."

"I don't know *much* about him."

"But you do know some things you haven't told me, don't you?"

"No. And why should you think I do?"

"Because you had a reason for going to Glenys' party; you need those upper class contacts. But what reason could she have for inviting you? Why does she need you?"

Jan stared at me silently.

"You admit you both hate each other," I pointed out.

She took a deep breath. "Maybe I add something. Maybe I'm the kind of person she likes to collect."

"Maybe. And you still cherish this great admiration for Roger Scott. Aren't you interested in knowing who killed him?"

She looked at me quietly and shook her head.

I ate some egg and toast.

"You don't trust anybody, do you?" she asked, after a few moments.

"I've never been suspicious of people until I opened the office. I've never had reason to be."

"But you're suspicious of me, now."

I said nothing. I didn't look at her.

"What was last night to you, just a frolic in the hay?"

I looked at her. "You tell me. And get that wronged woman look off your lovely face."

The blaze was back. "Get out of here. Damn you, get out of here."

I had a full cup of coffee in front of me and only half my three eggs eaten. But it didn't seem like a time to mention that.

I stood up and smiled down at her. I said, "I think you're one of the lambs, but let me remind you that the woods are full of tigers. You know who I am, now, and if you need me or want to help me, I'll come at your call."

I went back into the bedroom for my jacket, and out through the living room to a bright and hot morning. I wasn't happy; I liked Jan Bonnet. Through a wire mesh fence, a Doberman stared at me silently. He seemed to be quivering, though I couldn't be sure at this distance.

I stood next to the car a moment in indecision, and then realized she'd have one hell of a time getting to her car, public transportation being what it is in this town.

I went back up the slight slope to her house and looked in through the open upper half of the Dutch door. She was dialing the phone in the living room.

I called in, "I want to take you to your car."

She looked up, startled, and replaced the phone in the cradle. She stared at me. Then, finally, "There's no need of that. As a matter of fact, I—was just phoning a garage."

"I want to take you to your car," I repeated. "Let's not be adolescent."

She shook her head, stood up, and went back to the kitchen.

If she'd been dialing a garage, there'd have been no reason for her to stop dialing when I appeared. She must have been dialing a number she knew, for the phone book wasn't in sight, and she hadn't had time to look up a number in the seconds I'd been gone.

I was almost as close to Westwood as I was to my office; I went home and changed my clothes. The phone rang in the middle of that.

It was Glenys Christopher. "Well, you are a hard man to find, aren't you? I've been phoning your office and this number since nine o'clock."

"I'm a heavy sleeper," I said. "I didn't hear the phone."

"Perhaps you weren't close enough to it. They're hard to hear beyond a half a block or so."

I said nothing, waiting.

"Are you still there?"

"Yes, Miss Christopher. I'm waiting to learn why you phoned."

"You needn't be insolent, Brock Callahan."

"Yes, ma'm. Anything else, ma'm?"

A silence, and then, "No. Just this—forget our talk the other night about putting you on a retainer. I'll have no further need for your services." She hung up.

It didn't seem to be one of my better days with women. They have always been hard for me to figure and I guess I wasn't the only man in the world with that failing. I finished dressing and drove down to the office.

At the drugstore, I had the second half of my breakfast and two cups of coffee. My fan wasn't behind the counter this morning; the straw blonde who waited on me showed no indication of succumbing to the charm that had proved so fatal to Jan Bonnet.

Man-crazy, Glenys had called her. A sentimentalist. Jan had some opinions on Glenys, too. I still like Jan better. But maybe, if Glenys had been as kind—?

"More coffee?" the straw blonde asked indifferently.

I shook my head and took my check along to the cashier, another imitation blonde. The bleach industry must be a big one in this country.

My phone-answering service informed me that a Miss Christopher had phoned three times. There had been no other calls. I phoned the Venice Station and asked if the two hoodlums had been picked up.

They had been picked up and released, I was informed. They had denied slashing the upholstery. And as I didn't know the name of my witness to the act, there had been no grounds on which to charge the kids.

I phoned the West Side Station and got Dave Trask. There was nothing new. Nystrom had been released last night.

"On bail?"

"Mmmmm. No. We want him free and moving around, Brock. We have a theory on him."

I hung up and heard footsteps coming up the stairs. I went to the window and saw the Austin-Healey parked a half block down.

I was back in my chair, studying an insurance ad, when Bobby Christopher appeared in the doorway.

"Hi," I said. "You look fresh for a morning after."

"Why not? All I did was swim and eat hamburgers. Brock, what's with you and Sis?"

I shook my head. "Nothing. What do you mean?"

"What's she so furious about?"

"I don't know. Didn't she tell you?"

"Oh, come off it, Brock. I'm no baby. Was it because you took that Bonnet girl home?"

I held up a hand. "Just a minute, boy. Your sister was a client, not a guardian. She has no reason to concern herself with my social life."

"*Was* a client? Didn't she put you on a retainer?"

"We talked about it. This morning, she phoned and told me to forget it. And also that she had no further need for my services."

Bobby grinned. "Jealous. She sails for you, Brock."

"Now, you come off it. That's not my league. She could have her choice of dozens better."

Bobby's grin grew. "Modest, aren't you? You're not exactly homely, Callahan."

"Not exactly. But close enough. And you're too big to

be playing cupid. What kind of deal did you get from S.C.?"

Bobby sat down in my customer's chair and threw one leg over an arm of it. "Don't change the subject. Tell me about Glenys and you."

"Nothing," I said emphatically. "Nothing, nothing, nothing. You're way off base, Bobby, and I think this kind of talk is in poor taste."

His grin was a little strained. "All right, then, tell me about you and Jan Bonnet."

I said patiently, "Look, kid, it's been a messy day up to now. Don't make it any worse. Jan Bonnet is one of three people who attended Roger Scott's funeral. I thought she might be able to tell me something about him. She either can't or won't; she got indignant when I questioned her about him. She, like your sister, is not currently talking to Brock Callahan. I am now officially off the Roger Scott case. If you want to talk football, okay."

Bobby was no longer grinning. He said gravely, "Believe me, Brock, I know Sis. And she thinks one hell of a lot of you. And so do I, if that means anything to you."

"Thank you," I said. "Now tell me about S.C."

He stood up. "I don't want to talk football right now. I'm going to tell Sis she's stupid to let you go. I'm going to make her call you."

I smiled. "Okay. I can always use the business."

He smiled and waved. "See you." He went out and I heard his feet going down the steps.

I can use the business. . . . Who'd said that last night? Jan had said it to Glenys. From below came the sound of a horn, and I went to the window, but it wasn't anyone blowing for me. Up the block, I saw Bobby gun the Austin-Healey away from the curb.

Well, there wasn't any point in sitting around here; I

was still supposed to be working for Juan Mira. My phone rang, and it was the local Ford agency. The new seats were there.

They let me use a loaner while they worked on my car; I drove over to the West Side Station for a heart-to-heart talk with Dave Trask.

Trask looked tired but semi-friendly. He told me, "The girl has just disappeared. We've less than nothing on it. Nystrom we want to watch because we think he's organizing a new kind of crime element in this town."

"What kind?"

"Young hoodlums. The hot-rodders and the minority group punks who are spoiling for trouble, the petty thieves who are too young to know about fences they can trust, the broken-home girls who want to get paid for what they've been giving away. Nystrom could build some organization on that kind of material, couldn't he?"

"There wouldn't be much discipline," I said. "And he didn't seem like much of a brain to me."

"He's not long on brains, I'll grant you. But he's got one thing kids admire; he's got all the guts in the world. And don't think some of these hot-rodders aren't bright. When you can take a '34 Ford and run it up to over two hundred horsepower, you must have something above the neck. What sickens me is that kind of engineering genius going right down the drain to the cesspool."

Something came to me, and I voiced it. "You know, when Nystrom first saw me, he said he'd heard of me. Well, where would he hear about me—unless it was from those two hoodlums who cut up my upholstery?"

Dave Trask nodded. "Exactly. Ten minutes after those boys were brought into the Venice Station, there was a shyster down there to represent them. That kind of thing didn't used to happen. If we can break this up before

Nystrom is really organized, we'll save a hell of a lot of the taxpayer's money. That's why we let Nystrom go. We want to see who his adult contacts are."

I asked, "Do you think it would do us any good for me to talk to those kids?"

Trask stared past me, at the wall. "As a Ram, you mean? As a big local athlete?"

"Well, yes."

Trask sighed. "I don't know. There are kids who are impressed by that kind of reputation and kids who aren't. These kids weren't on your side when they went to work on your car. You can't approach 'em with any home, heaven and mother talk. That's for sure." He stood up and arched his back, as though stretching the aches out of it. "You're still a gringo to them, remember."

"So's Nystrom."

"Yup. But on the side of the fence they've picked for their own. Whatever you do, Brock, do it slowly. Don't go flexing your biceps at anybody."

"I promise. We're friends again, huh, Dave?"

"So long as you work with us. Though you're never going to be on Pascal's hit parade."

"I guess I can stand that," I answered. "I'll keep in touch."

He nodded. "That's the big thing—keep in touch with us."

I wasn't too far from Brentwood; I drove over to the motel. Randall was out in front, watering the parkway. He waved, as I drove up, and went to turn off the water.

When I came out of the car, he greeted me with, "What's new?"

"Nothing much. Anything new here?"

He shook his head. "I'm—waiting." He inclined his head toward the office. "Let's get out of the sun."

In his office, we enjoyed a moment of silence while he removed the cellophane wrap from a cigar. I had an impression he was thinking hard.

Finally, he said, "I suppose you work very closely with the police?"

"I was told a few minutes ago that that's the best way for me to stay in business."

Silence again.

So I said, "Was there something you wanted to tell me if I *didn't* work very closely with the police?"

"Well, now, Mr. Callahan, that's a hell of a way to put it."

I shrugged.

He looked out the window. "I've got fourteen units out there. Nobody gets rich on fourteen units."

"Even if they're constantly filled?"

"Even if they're constantly filled. And you can't keep them filled with tourists, not here. That's no national highway out there, it's no natural stopping place between big cities."

I smiled. "Mr. Randall, if you're working up to telling me that you get some quickie trade, don't you think you're laboring the obvious?"

He looked at me solemnly. He hadn't lighted the cigar; he was rolling it nervously between his fingers.

"Drop the other shoe, Mr. Randall," I said.

"And have Pascal blowing his breath in my face again?"

"That could be. But wouldn't you rather have Pascal on your neck than Nystrom?"

He lighted the cigar and blew out some smoke and watched it. His face looked guarded. "I really didn't have anything besides suspicion. The police don't want that, do they?"

"I think they might. There's very little else to go on in this mess."

"They got a fingerprint. That's something, isn't it? It doesn't match the maid's, or Scott's or that Rosa's. The technical man told me it was a very clear print, in blood, on one of the doors."

It was news to me. My friend, Trask.

Randall studied the end of his cigar. "What I didn't tell the police was my suspicion that Scott was running some kind of a racket in that room."

"You mean that Scott had been here before? I had the idea this was a one-night stand. He had an apartment in Hollywood, you know."

"I know. But he had that room on a retainer and he phoned me when he didn't intend to use it. And nights that he did have it in his name, he wasn't always the occupant."

A fine, white ash was growing on Randall's cigar. I thought I could smell the musky odor of sin in the Havana fragrance.

"Go on, Mr. Randall," I said.

He opened a drawer in his desk and brought out what looked like a photographic flash bulb, only it was coated with some dark substance.

"Infrared," he told me. "The maid would find them in the room some mornings."

"What are they used for?"

"For taking pictures in the dark with infrared film. The subject doesn't know he's being photographed."

"Or *she's* being photographed." I smiled. "You're not telling me Rosa Carmona could be blackmailed with compromising pictures? She'd probably use them for publicity. She wasn't in the kind of business where those kind of pictures would hurt her."

"Rosa, Rosa, Rosa," he said irritably. "She's missing, so the police make her the number one suspect. It gives them an out. What about that blonde with the yellow Plymouth? I gave them that, and what have they done with it?"

"I don't know. Nobody told me about her. The police don't always confide in me, Mr. Randall. What'd she look like?"

"Smallish woman. Beautiful build, fine clothes. She was here quite often. Used to come in the afternoons, once in a while, and wait for him."

"I see." I pointed to my loaner, out at the curb. "What kind of car is that, Mr. Randall?"

He stretched his neck to look out the window. "Dodge."

"What color?"

"Light green."

It was a light blue Ford six. I said, "Are you sure this yellow Plymouth wasn't a mustard-colored Chev?"

"Hell, yes. It was a hard-top. I saw it often enough."

"This Chev Bel Air is a hard-top, too."

"Mr. Callahan, I see cars all day long. Are you telling me I can't tell a Chev from a Plymouth?"

I shook my head. "No, but I'm telling you you can't tell a green Dodge from a blue Ford. That's a blue Ford at the curb."

"So I'm color-blind between green and blue a little. I knew that. And it's quite a distance to the curb from here. I saw the Plymouth a lot closer than this."

"You saw the Ford a lot closer than this, too. You were two feet from it when I got out of it."

"What the hell are we arguing about?" he asked irritably. "You got somebody special you want to nail?"

I shook my head. "But I know a smallish woman with a

beautiful build and fine clothes who knew Roger Scott.
And she drives a Chev Bel Air."

There was the sound of big tires on gravel, and a Cad
convertible came into our line of vision. Randall set the
cigar carefully on an ash tray, and went out. He took a
registry card along with him.

The driver was tall and tanned and blonde; the girl in
the seat beside him was tanned and bleached blonde. It was
a California license plate, and the frame around the plate
bore the insignia of a Beverly Hills dealer.

The Cad moved out of my line of vision, back toward
the units, and Randall came in with a ten dollar bill and
the registry card.

"Frisco people," he said. "We get a lot of them."

"Some drive, if they started this morning at a reasonable
hour."

He looked at me. "Not for a Cad. Those Cads eat a lot
of highway."

I made no comment.

He changed the subject. "This girl in the Plymouth—if
you know her, bring her around. I could maybe be wrong
about the car, but not about the girl. She's stuck in my
memory."

I nodded. "Could I have one of those burned-out flash
bulbs?"

He opened the drawer again and took one out. "Going
to give it to the police, are you?"

"I don't think so. Maybe you had better tell them about
it, though. There weren't any in the room the afternoon
the maid found Scott, were there?"

He shook his head. "That's why I didn't tell the police
about it."

That could have been *one* of the reasons. I thanked him
and went out to the hot car. I'd had a late breakfast but I

was getting a little hungry. It was now almost three o'clock.

Randall had withheld information from the police; I wondered how much he had withheld from me. If he had been in with Roger Scott on the photographic blackmail racket, it was likely that only the two of them knew of the connection. And Scott was dead; he couldn't implicate Randall.

It figured that Jan Bonnet could be a frequent visitor at the motel. She still carried the torch for Scott and she was not a phlegmatic woman. But whether she knew the true Scott, I couldn't be sure.

Nor whether I did, nor anyone else.

It didn't seem logical that an operator that smooth should get into a racket as cheap and vulgar as compromising photographs. There are too many unethical ways *within* the law for an operator like Scott to mint money. Why would he stick his neck out on anything as doubtful as blackmail?

My new upholstery was installed when I got back to Beverly Hills. The luncheon special was no longer in effect when I got to the drugstore. I ordered a steak sandwich and a salad and iced coffee.

The blonde was still behind the counter; the regular man was enjoying a da, at Hollywood Park, she told me.

The fat woman was back, digesting a *New Yorker*, this time, along with a four-scoop banana split smothered in pineapple, loaded with whipped cream.

My mind went to Jan Bonnet and clung there, reliving our mutual history from the funeral to the swim party to the half-eaten breakfast. A short and turbulent period that had been. Was the girl a tramp? I am no lure to the ladies; was the girl an indiscriminate, man-hungry tramp? I didn't want to think so.

And Glenys so indignant. . . . Why? There was a counter-length mirror here, showing me my undistinguished face. I am as vain as the next man, but the mirror assured me Glenys Christopher was not jealous.

Bobby was young and full of wishful thinking. To Bobby, any man under two hundred and thirty pounds who can play guard for the Rams is something special. I'd be the last to deny this, but the first to acknowledge that wouldn't make me the outsize Eddie Fischer for the distaff trade. The glamour of a football player fades for women after their college years.

Of course, in my way, I was a specialist, and Glenys collected specialists.

I had another glass of iced coffee and went up to the hot and airless office. There had been a call from a Miss Glenys Christopher, I was informed.

I didn't call back immediately. I opened all the windows and turned on the fan and sat down with a pitcher of water to type out my reports. I was making better time today, I'd added my thumb to the two active fingers, using the thumb for the space bar. I couldn't see why a man would have to go to business college to learn this.

At four-thirty I was finished, and I was about to file today's sheets when I decided to review them all, from the first day. Perhaps, in studying the sequence, I could get a picture, a pattern.

I studied them all. I even spotted my calls against a map of the L.A. metropolitan area, seeking some geographical clue to it all. Nothing came; I was more confused, if anything.

Well, what had I brought to this trade? Three years in the O.S.S. and my memories of a cop father. Along with a nodding acquaintanceship with maybe fifty lads in the Department. That didn't make me any Philip Marlowe.

Work alone wouldn't do it, nor determination; I was a

fraud in my chosen profession. So many are, but that didn't make me any more admirable.

At Redlands, Pool would be weeding the lambs from the goats, the men from the boys, the promising rookies from the broken hearts. One more year, maybe, and then some job I understood? Hamp would take me back for another year; he'd already told me that. I was no youngster, but I'd learned some tricks in the campaigns and I could get by for another year, maybe even two.

My bad knee worked well; all that bothered it was dampness. And the Rams were thin at guard.

My phone rang and I picked it up.

A rough voice said, "This is Nystrom, footballer. I'm just letting you know you won't get off so easy the next time we meet. If you're smart, you'll see we don't meet."

"Drop dead," I told him. "But thanks for calling, Red. You couldn't have picked a better time." I hung up on him.

CHAPTER EIGHT

I DIALED the Christopher residence and told the maid I was returning Miss Christopher's call. I heard the click of an extension phone being lifted and then Glenys', "Hello, Brock Callahan."

"Hello. You phoned?"

"To apologize. Bobby tells me I'm being unfair."

"He's partial to athletes," I said.

"Mmmmm-hmmm. Jan came for her car. She didn't bring a mechanic along."

I said nothing.

"We're friends again, aren't we, Brock?"

"If you want to be. I didn't know we ever were."

"Friends are what I need, *real* friends."

"Then I'm a friend. How much of a retainer did you have in mind?"

Silence for a moment, and then, "You can be cruel, can't you?"

"I can be tactless," I admitted. "To be truthful, I've been wondering whether I have anything to offer a client in this unusual profession."

"I think you have and I'm willing to put it into writing."

"Thank you, Glenys. I'll inquire from one of the big agencies as to a fair rate and have a contract drawn up. Your party was fun, last night."

"I'm glad you had fun. That wrestler was a mistake, though, wasn't he?"

"They usually are. But nobody got hurt. Bobby tells me he's going to S.C. Was that your school?"

"No. Smith. Will you be busy tonight?"

"I'm sorry. I will. Something important?"

"Nothing," she said, and there was a silence. Then, "Jan —?"

"No, I don't think so. The other end of town. I don't think Jan is involved too much in Roger Scott's death."

"Oh." A silence. "That wasn't exactly what I meant when I asked about her. What did you mean by 'the other end of town?' Did you mean East Los Angeles?"

"No. I meant financially, not geographically. I meant the other side of the tracks. Your friend mixed at all social levels, it seems."

"Roger—?"

"Right."

"I've stopped thinking of him as a friend. Call me tomorrow, won't you, Brock?"

"I will," I promised. "I'm glad we're friends again."

I hung up and went over to the mirror near the door, but the face was the same. I looked up Jan Bonnet in the phone book and found she had two addresses. The business address was only a few blocks from here.

It was almost five, but perhaps she kept her shop open until six. I didn't phone; I walked over there.

It was a narrow shop, sandwiched between a pair of women's apparel stores. *jan bonnett* in uncapitalized black script on the window and what looked like a wormwood front door.

It was cool and dim inside and Jan sat at the rear of the shop, in front of a desk and under a skylight. There were fabrics and wallpaper sample books all around on the library tables; there was a feeling of quiet elegance to the small place.

She looked at me wearily. "Well—? Good afternoon."

"Hello, Jan." I came over to where she sat and put the flash bulb on the small desk in front of her. "Know what that is?"

"It looks like a flash bulb. There's a photography shop three doors away. You could ask them."

"It is a flash bulb. Infrared. For taking pictures in the dark with infrared film."

She nodded. "I've heard of it. Didn't know the process was perfected though. Why are you showing it to me?"

"Because they were often found around Roger Scott's motel room. The manager, there, thinks that Scott used them for taking pictures. For blackmail purposes."

"That's ridiculous, of course."

"Is it, really?"

"It is to me."

"You spent a lot of time over there, Jan, didn't you? Over at that motel, I mean."

She stared at me, the brown eyes vulnerable. "Who told you that? Do the police know that?"

I shook my head. "The manager talked about a girl in a yellow Plymouth. That put the police off."

Here voice was low. "You're threatening me, aren't you? Why?"

"I'm not threatening you. You'd be the last I'd threaten, Jan, believe me. But why can't you be honest with me?"

"I don't know who killed Roger Scott. That is God's unvarnished truth, Brock Callahan. I don't know anything about infrared photography or blackmail. I was—infatuated with Roger, yes." She looked down at the desk top. "Maybe I infatuate easily; I can't seem to help being a woman." She looked up to face me candidly. "If you think I'm involved, take your information to the police. But please get out of here now."

"I thought I could buy a drink," I suggested. "We don't need to fight, Jan."

"We don't need to be friends, either," she said in a monotone. "I distrust your interest in me, Brock."

I studied her for seconds, trying to think of something to say, trying to find some opening through the wall.

"Get out," she said quietly. "Please get out."

I went out and over to the parking lot. I drove home slowly, thinking of them all. Randall was the most obvious phony in the cast; in the bright light of day he hadn't noticed any visitors to the room of Roger Scott. He hadn't noticed Rosa Carmona—he claimed. Randall wasn't necessarily implicated. He could be trying to protect his own reputation. So could they all, but in so doing, they were walling off the path to the killer.

At home, I took off my shoes and lay on the bed, staring at the ceiling and trying to think. Nothing bright came, and I dozed.

It was dark in the room when I wakened. The pillow was wet under the back of my neck and my clothes felt gummy. I turned on the light and saw that I had slept over three hours.

A shower, and three cool glasses of milk and then I put on a seersucker suit. For the wind was from the east and the heat would continue into the night. I considered taking a gun, and changed my mind.

The place was about half filled when I came in and the same big moose was behind the bar. He remembered me. He brought out a bottle of beer and looked at me questioningly.

I nodded, and he brought along a glass.

"That Richter's shaping up, I read. Good man, don't you think?" he asked.

"He'll be one of the great ones, like Don Paul."

"And Brock Callahan."

"Huh!" I said. "I'm a midget, next to those two."

"Cut it out," he said. "Name me a year you weren't an All-League choice."

I smiled, and said nothing, trying to look modest.

"I wish we'd have got Don Moomaw," he said.

I looked around, but there was no sign of Sue Ellen. A swarthy kid in jeans and T-shirt was putting dimes into the juke box, but when he turned away from it, I saw it wasn't one of the pair.

The bartender had gone down to the other end of the bar to serve a couple. I pushed a stool next to the wall at the end of the bar and sat on it, my back to the wall, my left elbow on the bar. I could see all of the room, now, and the small area that served as a stage.

The bartender finished serving the couple, and came back. "It looks like Detroit again this season, don't you think?"

"They're always tough," I said. "I'm a Ram fan, myself."

He nodded. "Who isn't, in this town?"

I asked, "Sue Ellen here?"

He shook his head. "She should be in soon, though." He looked at me doubtfully. "She's no relative, is she?"

I sipped my beer. "No. Why—?"

He shrugged. "I mean, you could do better than *that*. That's really a wretch without her make-up on." He seemed to shudder. "And the way she's been hitting the booze, she sure as hell ain't going to get any prettier."

"Just *lately*, she's been hitting the booze?"

He nodded. "The last couple of days. And she's nervous as a cat until she's loaded. Then she gets gabby."

"Maybe she's frightened of something—or somebody."

"Maybe. She keeps it up, she'll get the can for sure. And where can you go from here?"

A guitar player and an accordionist came in from the

back hallway now and took their chairs near the piano.
Then the front door opened, and Sue Ellen came in.

She looked haggard and nervous. Her glance moved
along the bar, paused at me. Indecision fought a losing
battle on her face, and she came my way.

"Don't leave," she told me quietly. "I want to talk to
you, later."

I smiled. "All right, Sue Ellen. I'll wait." I tried to look
as friendly as possible.

She went down the hallway toward her dressing room.
The piano player took his seat at the piano and the
three of them went to work on *Carolina Moon*. They went
from that to some Spanish music, and then Sue Ellen made
her entrance, to a trickle of applause.

She sang a double-entendre bit about *Daddy's Not As
Old As All That* and the applause was stronger. She went
lower with a *Southern Girl Who Didn't Know The Way*
and I was uncomfortable. But evidently the audience had
less shame; they loved it.

Then her whiskey contralto took them all into the gutter
with a pornographic ditty usually reserved for stags or a
Las Vegas audience. There is no law in Vegas; hoodlums
own and run that town. But I was surprised the L.A.P.D.
would let this kind of thing go on in Venice.

Next to me, the bartender shook his head.

"Me, too," I said. "But who are we, against so many?"

Sue Ellen went by and gestured. I followed her down
the hall.

Into the odor of perspiration and talcum powder and it
seemed to intensify as she closed the door behind us. She
pointed to a battered kitchen chair and sat down in front
of her dressing table, with her back to it.

"I have to talk to somebody," she said. "You're working
for Mira, aren't you?"

I nodded.

"And with the police?"

I hesitated, and nodded.

A pause, and then, "Rosa didn't phone you that day at your office. I did."

"And imitated Rosa's voice?"

"I didn't need to. I just changed my own. You didn't know what her voice sounded like."

"Why did you do that?"

"Because we knew the manager kept a record of calls and this would make it look like Rosa was in the motel at that time."

"And why did you want that established?"

"Because I was conned into thinking it would throw Mira off the trail. I knew how Rosa wanted to get rid of him, and Red told me this would do it, would throw you off."

"Red—? Red Nystrom?"

"Who else?"

I said, "Roger Scott was in that room, *dead*, when you phoned, Sue Ellen."

"That's what I read in the papers, now. But believe me, he wasn't anywhere in sight when I phoned you."

"That call would make Rosa a suspect for the murder."

"Don't I know it? Damn it, don't I know it, *now*?"

"Nystrom took you over there?"

She nodded.

"Didn't the manager see you?"

She shook her head. "That room of Scott's is in the rear and if you park on the side street, there, you can walk right across to it without anybody seeing you."

"Nystrom killed Scott, then?"

She shrugged. "I don't know. He doesn't seem like the kind who'd use a knife, does he?"

"He had a beef with Scott, though. He threatened him. The manager heard that a few days before."

"I suppose he wanted to cut in on Scott's racket. I guess Rosa was working with Scott on that, whatever it was."

I nodded. "And those two punks who were in here the other afternoon—they work for Nystrom, too, do they?"

"They know him—that much I know. Say, you don't think those two—" She stared at me, horror in her eyes.

"Nystrom's working with the young ones," I said. "And the way they worked my upholstery over—" I shrugged.

"Upholstery's one thing. But a man—Jesus, Callahan, you can't believe—" She shook her head. "I need a drink. Will you get me a drink?"

I got her some bourbon over ice and came back. She was smoking a cigarette. She had taken her shoes off.

I handed her the drink, and asked, "Where's Rosa now, Sue Ellen?"

"I wish to God I knew. I wish to God I knew if she was even alive."

"Nystrom must have killed Scott," I said, "and then tried to frame Rosa for it. But why Rosa?"

"Who knows? Gawd, the guts of the man, huh? Taking me into that room. How the hell could he know he wouldn't be seen?"

"Red's not short on guts," I said. "Sue Ellen, you've got to tell this to the police."

"I know," she said. "But not yet. Give me time to line up some friends."

"The police will protect you."

"No thanks. I can find better protection than that. I know who to go to, but it'll take time. Red's too wild and loud to suit the big boys on this side of the fence. But I want *them* to take care of him, not the police."

"Nobody scares Red," I argued. "He's too damned dumb to be scared by the big boys. You'd better come over to the law's side, and quickly, Sue Ellen."

She shook her head. "Not yet. And I'll call you a liar if you tell them what I told you."

"Who do you think the police would believe?"

She finished her drink. "I've a few connections, Callahan. I wasn't always this unattractive. Don't cross me, or you'll regret it."

"Then why did you tell me this?" I asked.

"Because of Rosa. She's the best friend I ever had. And I hoped it would help you find her."

"And now you've told me all you know?"

"Every bit of it. Would you get me another double bourbon? That bartender makes cracks when I buy them."

She went over to open the small window as I went out with her glass.

I was about halfway along the hall when I heard the smashing explosion behind me. From the barroom came screams and I turned back toward the small dressing room.

The window was open; Sue Ellen was on her back, her face almost completely shot away. The stink of gunpowder filled the room and I paused for a moment.

Only a shotgun at close range could have done that damage. I hoped he didn't have a repeater, as I went to the window and looked out.

It was an alley, and there was a light at the far end. I saw the man running. I saw the fringe of red hair around the bald pate and the ridiculous skinny legs and the enormous shoulders. I saw the shotgun in his hand, and though I couldn't be sure, it didn't look like a repeater.

Big stupid hero, Brock Callahan, went out the window and after him.

CHAPTER NINE

I CURSED myself for not having brought a gun, as I'd planned. Running down the alley, toward the light at the corner, I looked for cover I could use in case Red Nystrom stopped running.

I came to the street end, and hesitated.

Then I heard the sound of straight tail-pipes blasting and the screech of a souped car getting underway under full gun. I came out to the street just in time to see a chopped and channeled '34 Ford coupe go screaming around the next corner. I couldn't make out the license number.

I came back into the bar the front way, and a woman pointed at me and screamed, "That's him, that's him—"

The bartender shouted, "Shut up, all of you! I've phoned the police. This man's a cop."

A man near the doorway who'd lifted a chair set it down again and smiled shakily. I went to the phone and asked for the West Side Station.

Pascal wasn't there, nor Caroline, nor Trask. They were off duty. Captain Apoyan happened to be in, and I finally got through to him.

I told him what had happened, and suggested he call Trask. I finished the call as the uniformed men from the prowl car arrived. They were followed, a few minutes later, by a detective from the Venice Station. By the time Trask and Pascal got there, the ambulance had come and gone.

The patrons had been shooed out by this time, but they were still outside and blocking traffic. The barroom was filled with photographers and reporters.

Flash bulbs popped and reporters yacked and the cops

grumbled. Pascal and Trask took me into the room where Sue Ellen had died.

"You'd go into court and swear it was Nystrom?" Trask asked me.

"I didn't see his face. I saw that build of his and the red fringe on top. There aren't many men who look like he does."

"That still wouldn't be enough. How about the car?"

"I didn't get the license number. It was a black '34 Ford coupe. Chopped and channeled, with twin tail-pipes."

"That's the kind those two hoodlums drive," Pascal said.

"And dozens of others," I said. "It's a popular model. I thought you guys had a tail on Nystrom."

Trask didn't answer that. He shook his head and rubbed one cheek tiredly. "We know it's Nystrom. But we can't sentence people. Will the judge accept it, or a jury?"

"I haven't told you all of it," I said. I went on to tell them the story Sue Ellen had given me before she'd died.

Dave Trask looked less tired. "Well, now, that's a little better. We take that into court and—" He looked at me meaningly. "—your memory gets a little better, we've got a case. You saw his face, all right, didn't you?"

I shook my head.

Pascal said contemptuously, "A square we've got, Lieutenant. We all know it's Nystrom. We'd all stake our lives on it. But Callahan, he likes to see guys like that run loose. What's justice to a hairsplitter like Callahan?"

I looked at Pascal. "You're too far gone to have me explain justice to you, Sergeant. By the time you get through with Red, he'll probably confess to starting the Civil War. You don't need me."

"Shut up, both of you," Trask said irritably. "We'll get around to you, Brock, after we catch Nystrom. How come this Sue Ellen tells you things she didn't tell the police?"

I said, "She had an unwarranted lack of faith in the police, for some reason. I told her she'd better bring it right to you and she told me she had better connections than that to take it to. I would have told you, of course."

"Of course," Pascal said.

"Lieutenant," I said quietly, "get that son-of-a-bitch out of my hair."

Trask said, "Watch your language, Brock." He looked at Pascal and back at me. "Who were the connections?"

"I don't know. They must have been hangovers from a happier time, because she explained that she hadn't always been this unattractive. The only reason she opened up to me is because she knew I was looking for Rosa, and she was a friend of Rosa's."

"You're armed?"

I shook my head.

"And you went down that alley after a man with a gun?"

"It was a shotgun, and it didn't look like a repeater."

"It could have been a double-barreled shotgun. Could you see it that well?"

I shook my head.

Trask shook his, too. "Amateurs—You're the luckiest man in the world. What brought you over here tonight?"

"My search for Rosa Carmona. This seemed to be the best place to concentrate on."

Pascal said, "How do we know he wasn't fingering the girl for Nystrom?"

Trask frowned. "Slow up, Sergeant. Drop it." He turned back to me. "Okay, Brock. Come in tomorrow and make out your statement. Get there by ten. And if you've got any sense, you'd better wear a gun until we find Red Nystrom. And don't go down any dark streets."

In the hallway, flash bulbs popped and a pair of reporters

blocked my passage. "What's the story, Callahan?" one of them asked.

"The lieutenant has it," I told them. "He asked me not to talk to the press."

"To hell with him. He's not giving us orders, Callahan."

I nodded sadly. "But he's giving me orders. I don't have a powerful job, like you fellows."

"C'mon, Callahan," one of them said, but I shouldered my way past and got through the barroom without being accosted.

The night was still warm. The crowd was in knots on the sidewalk here and across the street. A uniformed man was keeping Main Street traffic from turning down this way.

I had the jitters. I sat in the Ford for seconds, afraid to turn on the key. Then I finally got a flashlight and opened the hood to check the motor. Nothing had been gimmicked; no bombs were in evidence.

Getting in, again, I looked in the back seat and found nothing. *Too many B pictures, Callahan,* I told myself. I turned on the radio, and drove past the gesturing policeman, back toward home. There was no reason to scorn myself: a wild man like Red Nystrom carrying a shotgun is a threat to consider.

He was no suave Las Vegas hoodlum working the angles, mixing with the pseudo-elite, wearing Hollywood strip tailoring. He was a direct and violent man and not open to pressure or reasoning. His was the tornado approach. And he had the wild, young punks behind him who played the way he did.

Young savages in the geranium jungle, spawned by uncaring parents in the pause between wars. Born in the depression and hating the world now growing rich on defense spending, minority group toughies who meant to get theirs, one way or another.

Red knew just enough to keep them loyal, the shysters, the quack doctors, the better-paying fences. Red would see that they got the best deal they could on that side of the law.

The radio music came on softly. It was only about eleven o'clock, but most of the houses were dark, the solid citizens in bed. While the young wolves prowled.

I was hungry. I pulled into a drive-in on Olympic and went inside to eat. I tried to blank the face of Sue Ellen from my mind and the memory of that big-shouldered man running down the alley with a shotgun in his hands.

Outside, I heard the rumble of a steel-packed muffler and I flinched, my nerves twitching. In a circular booth, some square-dancers were gabbing happily, in a world of their own.

Two hamburgers later, my stomach felt better, but my nerves were still jumpy. I nursed a cup of black coffee and thought back on the past three days.

It was logical to suspect Scott's death could be connected to Red, one way or another. I was sure in my own mind that Red had killed Sue Ellen; whether I'd swear to it in court or not. Which left me with my original pursuit, the finding of Rosa Carmona.

I wondered, if I hadn't gone out for Sue Ellen's drink, if I, too, would now be on a morgue slab? The window had been partially open when I'd left the room, if my memory hadn't failed. Had Sue Ellen gone over to open it wider or had she seen the killer out there?

I doubted that Red had been listening, or he would have sent me into eternity with Sue Ellen. She'd been the weak link in his chain and Red had a standard remedy for that.

He probably didn't know I'd gone out the window after

him. If he learned it, through the newspapers, his primitive mind might consider me a threat.

The flivver took me home without comment and went to sleep with a sigh in the garage. There were night shadows in the court as I went up the iron steps. Somewhere a baby cried and a garbage grinder whirred.

Outside my door, I paused. I don't remember ever having paused there before. When I went in, I snapped the light on quickly. My apartment was vacant and innocent and hot.

I bathed my face with cool water and sat up for a while, trying to read the paper. But emotional fatigue took over; I was yawning and nodding within a half hour.

In the morning, the *Times* gave it the full front page treatment. There were pictures of Sue Ellen and of me and of Red Nystrom. It must have been an old picture of Red; he had all his hair. An extensive search was being made for him.

Which made two the police were seeking, Red and Rosa. And gave them a hotter prospect for the gas chamber than they'd had in Rosa. Whether Red had killed Scott or not might not matter too much; if he was gassed for Sue Ellen's death, they could write off Scott on him, too. Randall would testify that Red had threatened Scott, and I would testify as to what Sue Ellen told me. Very few juries would split hairs over Red Nystrom.

My phone rang and I answered it. The voice was masculine, genial and confident. "Mr. Brock Callahan?"

"Speaking."

"My name is Wendell Lange, Mr. Callahan. I'm an attorney, with offices in Hollywood, here, and I wondered if it would be possible for me to see you some time this morning?"

"What about, Mr. Lange?"

"Well, it so happens that I frequently have need of a capable private investigator, Mr. Callahan. There is no such need at the moment but if you aren't busy, it could be to your future advantage to drop in for a little—chat, shall we say?"

"Could you make it this afternoon, Mr. Lange? I think my morning is going to be taken up."

"This afternoon will be fine. Shall we say two o'clock?"

"Two o'clock will be fine. What is the address?"

He gave it to me, and I hung up, trying to think where I'd heard of that name. The famous lawyers in this area are divorce lawyers and I was sure he wasn't one of those.

At the West Side Station, where I filled out my statement, Dave Trask enlightened me.

"Criminal lawyer," he said. "He never got the big boys' business, but he's represented a lot of the independent hoods, the mavericks. He's handled enough of them to make a fair reputation for himself."

"Why do you think he wants to see me?"

"To find out how much you know about Red Nystrom. Why else?"

"How much do I tell him?"

Dave looked at me thoughtfully. "Are you asking for instructions?"

"In a way. What if he asks me if I really saw Red Nystrom last night?"

"You can tell him the same thing you told us. That's the truth, isn't it?"

I nodded. "And that's what you want me to tell him?"

"Why not? We want Red to stay around town. And if we haven't got a witness who can *positively* identify him, he will stay around town."

"And if you haven't got a witness like that, what good will it do you to pick him up?"

Trask smiled. "We have some pretty good lawyers on our side, too. Men who know how to build a case for a jury or a judge. If you were on a jury and Nystrom was brought before you, how would you vote?"

"I don't know, Dave. I'd have to give it more thought than I have."

"You wouldn't be picked for our jury, then. Keep in touch with us, Brock. Let me know what Lange tells you."

I promised I would, and went out into a day about fifteen degrees cooler than yesterday. Yesterday, instead of booking Red, he'd been released. Because they'd wanted him free and moving around, as Dave had said.

Because of that, Sue Ellen was now dead. And I hadn't noticed any signs of a strained conscience on the face of Lieutenant Dave Trask. There couldn't be, in his business. It was no trade for introverts or philosophers. The decisions came piling up, one on the other, and they had to be made against the exigencies of the moment. If they weren't made, and quickly, the machinery of the law would halt and the hoodlums would be in complete command.

Criminal lawyers knew that and they used it for making their "deals," for getting a prosecutor to water down the charge in return for the criminal's admission of guilt to the lesser charge. That kept the courts from being swamped with legal tangles that would put the calendar years behind. It changed justice from a finely balanced scale to a quick rule of thumb decision. It occasionally resulted in some spectacular miscarriages which the newspapers loved to belabor.

But none of the critics could come up with a better solution. The original crime was society's, not the law's. The law didn't even get to them until society had perverted them.

There was a reporter waiting in front of my office door. He was from the *Times* and he wanted more than the others had been given last night.

"This is headline stuff, Callahan, and you're right in the middle of it. Don't you think the public's entitled to some facts?"

"I've just filled out my statement at the West Side Station," I told him. "I'll let Lieutenant Trask decide how much the public's entitled to."

"I see. You're playing Pontius Pilate, is that it?"

I smiled at him. "And you're playing God. Who are you to judge what the public's entitled to know?"

"I'm the guy who tells them."

"And I'm a guy who likes to eat. And in order to eat, I have to get along with the police. That's clear enough, isn't it?"

"It's clear enough for me," he said. "When you opened this office, you stopped being a citizen." He left me on that line.

Fine, brave words, but the reality was that the *Times* had its own evaluation of the news and on its scale, Hedda Hopper ranked considerably above any trivial facts that might be coming out of the U.N. or Europe or Asia. The *Times* didn't even know what to do with the news it did receive.

There was no mail of any importance. I phoned Juan Mira.

His voice was plaintively hopeful. "You find my Rosa?"

"No, Juan, I haven't. Have you read the morning papers?"

"Yes. The old bag got hers, huh?"

"Do you know Red Nystrom?"

"No. He's got my Rosa?"

"I doubt it. But he might know something about her. That wasn't Rosa who phoned me that day from the motel; it was Sue Ellen."

"So—?"

"So Red brought Sue Ellen over there for that job. And now he's killed her, I'm sure. I hoped you might know something about him."

"Nothing. He is rich, this Nystrom?"

"Not that I know of. Why?"

"If he is not rich, the police will find him. Then we will learn what happened to Rosa. You want more money?"

"I've plenty, Juan. I haven't done you much good so far, have I?"

"I am not kicking. Keep looking, Brock Callahan."

I phoned Glenys and her voice sounded tight, strained. "Migawd, you went through something last night, didn't you?"

"It was pretty rough," I admitted. "I guess those are the perils of this trade."

"And you went out after him, after a man carrying a shotgun."

"I'm a little punchy," I admitted. "How did you first get to know Jan Bonnet?"

A momentary silence. "Let's see—I think it was through Les Hartley. He's an interior decorator, too. Though I can't believe Jan would be really interested in him."

"Why not?"

"Well, Les is—I mean, girls are not for him. And, of course, Jan is—I mean, she's *all* woman, which I'm sure you know, and—Oh heavens, why all this interest in Jan Bonnet?"

"Because I have a feeling she knows more than she's telling me. She was very close to Roger Scott."

"I can imagine. Have you two fought?"

"She's not speaking to me at the moment."

Another silence, longer this time. Then, "To tell you the truth, Brock, I'm really no longer interested in who killed Roger Scott. And I'm sure **we** can both agree that Jan is no criminal."

"Not a professional criminal, you mean. All right, Glenys; you asked me to call today, and I did. I'll get that contract drawn up."

"I'll be waiting for it," she said, which could have had meaning or could have been meaningless. I decided it was the latter.

The special was wieners and kraut; I had a steak sandwich and a milk shake. The counterman was full of woe; the horses had given him a licking yesterday. He bent my ear with the story of his financial fall.

I was glad to get away. From a booth, I phoned Wendell Lange and asked if it would be all right for me to come in a little early. It was only one o'clock.

"Fine," he said. "I'll be waiting."

That made two of them. I was over there ten minutes later.

The offices were large and clean, but more utilitarian than ornamental. The large reception room also contained the files and all the files were locked.

The receptionist was a scrubbed young woman with severe hair styling and horn-rimmed glasses. She ushered me into Lange's office as soon as I identified myself.

He sat behind a gray-enameled steel desk in a room with gray carpeting and gray walls. He could have been a warden or a conservative politician.

He had a well-shaped head on a rangy body. He had a close-cut crop of gray-black hair and cold blue eyes. He stood up to shake my hand and sat down again. The scrubbed girl left the room, closing the door quietly behind her.

I said, "Doesn't your office scare away clients?"

He frowned. "I don't understand, Mr. Callahan."

"It has a prison feeling," I said. "All the gray and the lack of ornament."

His smile was cool. "I never thought of it. I'm partial to gray, I guess. I see you've beeen inquiring about me."

I said nothing.

"Lieutenant Trask, no doubt?"

I nodded.

He locked his long, bony fingers together and leaned forward on the steel desk. "Frankly, my major concern was Red Nystrom, but I *do* need an investigator from time to time."

"I can't help you with Red Nystrom," I told him. "I don't know where he is."

"But you know where he was last night?"

"I think we both know that."

He shook his head. "I don't. Are you sure it was Red who killed that girl?"

I hesitated—and shook my head.

He leaned back in his chair. "Well—? And yet the papers are screaming for his scalp this morning and there is an extensive police search for him. Doesn't it frighten you, Mr. Callahan, this hounding of an untried man?"

I shook my head. "You frighten me, though, a man who spends all that time in law school just to learn how to circumvent the law."

His smile was tolerant and patronizing. "You're not a lawyer, Mr. Callahan?"

I shook my head.

"I didn't think so. Lawyers have more concern for the law. Your concern is probably with your idea of what is called justice. That's a word open to too many interpretations. I'm content to operate within the law."

I smiled at him. "At least when you have to. Don't you think it was deceitful to get me up here on the pretext of hiring me, when all you wanted to know was the case against Red Nystrom?"

"You're guessing, again," he said. "You're judging without a trial. Facts, facts, facts—that's what the law deals with, Mr. Callahan."

"All right, here are a couple. Red Nystrom tried to muscle me at that motel. He phoned me and threatened me. You know and I know he's knee-deep in murder. If you had as much concern for the law as you claim to have, you'd turn him over to the police, right now."

"Mr. Callahan, my first duty is to my client."

"Well, my first duty is to the law. So I guess we've no ground to meet on, have we?" I stood up.

He looked at me thoughtfully. "You're new to your trade, aren't you? You've a lot to learn, Mr. Callahan. I could be very valuable to you."

"I hope you never will be," I said. "I hope things never get that rough."

He sighed, and stood up. His smile was distant. "Are you annoyed because the police have no case against Red? Are you petulant because your conscience won't permit you to railroad a man you personally dislike?"

"That could be it," I said, and grinned at him. "You can deliver him to the law, now, Mr. Lange. There's no case against him."

The thin smile faded and doubt came to his cold eyes. "You've been briefed, haven't you? You came up here to lay a trap."

I grinned some more. "I can not swear on the witness stand that the man I saw running down that alley was

Red Nystrom. Isn't that what you wanted to hear?"

"But there's more you're not telling me."

I shook my head.

"You talked to this Sue Ellen, didn't you, before she was shot?"

That hadn't been in the papers. I said, "Not that evening, Mr. Lange."

Which was a lie, but a lie is concerned with justice, not the law. Wendell Lange's declared dedication was to the law.

"Are you lying?" he asked me.

"Lieutenant Trask has my statement," I said. "If he wants to release it, he will."

The blue eyes were indignant. "You came here in bad faith, Mr. Callahan."

"I came here at your request. You lied to get me here. My stomach won't permit me to stay any longer. Good day, Mr. Lange." I gave him my proud and honorable back and marched out to the sound of unheard trumpets.

CHAPTER TEN

IN THE BIG waiting waiting room, the receptionist was taking off an earphone. She had a short-hand notebook on the desk in front of her.

I asked, "Did you get it all? I hope I didn't speak too fast for you."

Some color in the scrubbed face.

"He must pay well," I said.

She looked at me coolly. "Adequately. Was there something else, Mr. Callahan?"

"Nothing." I stood a moment, looking at her.

Her chin lifted, and she faced me defiantly. "Mr. Callahan, you are now in Hollywood. Adjust!"

"Yes'm," I said humbly, and went out.

It was a little after one-thirty and I couldn't think of a place to go. The flivver seem to steer itself back to Beverly Hills and to an open spot at the curb in front of the shop of Jan Bonnet.

The wormwood door opened, and a stout woman came out. I waited a few moments, and then went in.

Jan was in rough linen, today, black and yellow, the hair severely back and in a horse's tail. Outdoorsy, with *Vogue* overtones.

"You—" she said.

"The persistent suitor. Have you read the morning papers?"

She nodded. "A regular Tarzan, aren't you? All muscle and no sense."

"Have you had lunch?"

"I was just going out. Something I could show you?"

"That eyetooth. It fascinates me."

She stood erectly, her arms stiffly at her sides. "Why all the persistence, Mr. Callahan? Because I'm—*easy?* Because you think I'm a round-heels?"

"You need to be slapped," I said. "That was vulgar."

"All right then, *why*—? Because I was a friend of Roger Scott's?"

I said earnestly, "Only because I thought you were a friend of mine. I promise not to bother you again."

I did the big turn, toward the door and took two slow steps, waiting for the call. But she waited until I had my hand on the knob and the door partially open.

Then she said, "All right, you bum. You can cut out the theatrics."

I turned back, smiling. "I'll buy you a lunch any place you want it. And you can direct the conversation."

"I'll go. *But just tell me why.*"

"You're attractive," I said, "but I don't think it's love, yet. I honestly don't know, Jan. Do I have to have reasons to like you?"

She sniffed. "You do like me?"

"Of course. And you know it. Everybody likes you, I'll bet. You're so—so genuine. Why, you don't even dye your hair."

"I'm thinking of it," she said. "I'll be with you in a minute."

She went through a door in the rear wall of the shop, and I leafed through the books of wallpaper samples. That proved dull, and I went over to finger the fabrics.

I heard Jan laugh and turned back to see her standing in the doorway she'd gone through.

"You're certainly a strange one," she said. "Why were you doing that?"

"I don't know. I have to be doing something. I can't seem to sit and do nothing."

"You and Bobby Christopher," she said. "Is it the athlete's cross, or something?"

"Maybe. Bobby's going to S.C. That kid could make it in his sophomore year, I'll bet."

"Make what?"

"All-American. He's the hottest prep-school prospect in ten years out here."

She shook her head. "All that and All-American, too. Do you like *Cini's?*"

"I've never been there," I told her. "Remember, I'm new to Beverly Hills."

A small and quiet place and she had spaghetti Neapolitan with Chianti and I had a pizza. I didn't want to tell her I'd already had lunch; it might seem to indicate I was hounding her.

The place was quiet and the cushioned booth soft and Jan pleasant to look at. It probably wasn't the time or the place to talk about murder.

But I said, "Glenys tells me she's no longer interested in who killed Roger Scott."

Nothing from Jan.

"When she first came into my office," I ploughed on, "she told me she was vitally interested and she was also frightened. I can't understand her change in attitude."

Jan's voice was soft. "Are you questioning me, Brock Callahan, or making casual conversation?"

"I don't honestly know," I said. "And I guess I haven't any reasons for worrying about Roger Scott if Glenys hasn't. The man's dead and he was no friend of mine. I didn't even know him."

Jan sipped her coffee, not looking at me.

I sipped my coffee and looked at her. "I should think you'd be happy about my suspicions of Glenys Christopher."

"I've had a lot of business through Glenys. I don't really hate her. I think I pity her."

"Don't hand me that poor-little-rich-girl line."

"All right, I won't. Glenys would give every nickel of it to be talented in some way, though."

"Would you trade with her?"

Jan shook her head. "I eat, Callahan. And get an occasional compliment. And create some beauty, here and there. I'm content."

"You should be married, a sweet girl like you."

She smiled at me. "Is that an offer?"

"Fatherly advice. Then, when this great therapeutic need hits you, you'd have your own medicine chest."

"Easy, Callahan," she warned me.

"I'm surprised Glenys hasn't married," I said. "She's pretty, and rich, too."

"And suspicious, too. So many smart, rich girls are." She looked at her watch. "I've a two-thirty appointment. We must flee, Callahan."

At the door of her shop, where I left her, I said, "When you need a—a friend, I hope you'll think of me, Jan Bonnet."

"Corny but sweet," she said. "I'll keep your name on file." She patted my cheek and went through the wormwood door.

I'd meant to ask her more, but she wasn't a girl you could crowd. We were friends, again, and there'd be another time and I could hope she'd be less defensive.

And then the obvious came back to me again, and I wondered if I'd mentioned it to Dave Trask. I went back to the office and phoned him and caught him in.

I said, "These two hoodlums who cut up my upholstery —have they been fingerprinted?"

"No. I don't even know their names."

"The Venice Station would have the names. I was thinking about that one good fingerprint you found."

"Who told you about that?"

"You didn't, did you? Why didn't you, Dave?"

"I asked you a question, Brock."

"I think Randall told me," I said, "though I'm not sure." Silence, and then, "What did Wendell Lange have to say this afternoon?"

"He gave me a lecture on the difference between justice and the law. I told him I couldn't be sure of Red, but he's still suspicious that you boys know more than you're releasing to the papers."

"Did he get that suspicion from you?"

"I don't think so. His office girl made a transcription of our conversation. You could ask him for it."

"I see. Anything else?"

"There was a *Times* reporter waiting at my office for me this morning."

"And what did you tell him?"

"That you had my statement and would release it when you saw fit. He lectured me, too. I get a lot of lectures, even outside the Department. But not much respect from anybody."

A chuckle, and then, "You pore little fella—you're being abused, aren't you?"

"I certainly am. Well, I don't mean to hold up a big, busy official like you, Dave. I won't do it again." I hung up.

My phone rang almost immediately, but I didn't answer it. I went down to the flivver and turned it toward Venice. I should have stayed with the Rams. In that trade, even lovable Ed Sprinkle had respected me. He should have; I'd knocked him on his ass often enough.

The flivver murmured consolingly. The sun tried to come out from the low overcast. I heard the bark of a rod

in the lane to my left, and stole a glance in the side mirror.
It was a converted Merc, and my breath came easier.

I had a small, nagging ache under my eyes which felt
like bad teeth but was probably sinusitis. The farther west
I traveled, the cooler was the air coming through the inlets.
I closed the left hand one, and stopped at a drugstore in
Santa Monica. I bought a box of aspirin and asked for a
glass of water at the fountain.

Looking back on my pursuit objectively, I felt there
wasn't too much reason to be dispirited. I had helped the
police, whether Trask would admit it, or not. Sue Ellen
had told me things she might never have told them, and
I'd been the first to guess at the tie-up between Red
Nystrom and the hoodlums.

And I knew who the girl in the supposed yellow Plymouth was. But I hadn't given that to Trask. I was playing it the Wendell Lange way, there. And why? What
was she to me?

She was pretty and emotionally erratic and probably
talented but she wasn't any one-man girl, not Jan Bonnet.
Why should I stick my neck out protecting her? Simply
because she was vulnerable, a lamb among wolves? I didn't
know that she was, not for sure.

She had stuck her own neck out, a little, going to the
funeral of Roger Scott. If I did tell Trask about her, he
could use that as an excuse for interrogating her; he
wouldn't have to tell her that I'd been the finger. But could
I trust Trask? He didn't trust me.

I kept telling myself.

For that matter, Glenys Christopher hadn't been questioned by the police, either. And she'd been a friend of
Scott's. And she'd hired me right after she'd read about
the murder and my part in it. That had been awful damned
coincidental.

Venice isn't far from Beverly Hills as the vulture flies, but it's a million miles away on the social register map. What was the connection here?

One came to me and made me gasp, mentally. I laughed at it, but it came back, bolstered by attitudes and fitting into the picture.

You're reaching for the moon, Callahan, I told myself. *There hasn't been a shred of evidence to support this ridiculous guess.*

My bartender fan was just coming on duty. He looked at me doubtfully. "I should think you'd have a bellyfull of this place. Haven't you got *any* nerves?"

"I've been thinking of Rosa Carmona," I said. "Do you remember when she worked here?"

"Sure do. If it hadn't been for that little boy friend of hers, she'd still be working here."

"A major attraction, eh?"

He nodded. "And to all kinds. We got some carriage trade, believe it or not, when that doll worked here."

"I wondered," I said, "if you remember—"

The door opened, and we looked that way and I stopped talking. One of the hot-rodders was standing there, the door still open behind him.

"I've been looking for you, footballer," he said. "They picked up my buddy."

"Who picked him up, son?" I asked calmly.

"The cops. You fingered him, huh?"

I shook my head. "How come they didn't pick you up, too?"

"I wasn't around where they could get me."

"How do you know he was picked up, then?"

The door closed behind him, now, and he came my way. He had his right hand in his trousers pocket.

I hadn't brought a gun. Trask had warned me, but I

hadn't brought a gun. I watched him as he came closer.

I said quickly, "That's close enough. Stay where you are, boy." I reached under my jacket, faking it.

His brown eyes were scornful. "I watched you come in. I can tell when a man's wearing a gun. Pull it out, if you've got one."

His hand came out from the pocket and it held a clasp knife. He pressed a button and the blade flicked open. He held it low, cutting edge up.

I said softly, "Don't be a damned fool, kid. You're clear, up to now."

He smiled. "Keep talking, footballer."

"Red hasn't got enough strings out," I said. "He's small-time and stupid. He can't do you any good on a big rap."

"Who mentioned Red?" he asked me. "I want to know about my buddy."

"I'll call the police and ask them," I offered. "I don't know why they want him. But I could phone."

"Don't whine, footballer. Just talk."

The bartender moved a hand toward the phone and the brown eyes flicked his way. The bartender brought his hand back. He gulped.

"Talk, damn you," the young hoodlum said.

"To hell with you," I said. "You come for me with that knife and I'll make you wish you were dead, punk. Now put it away." I edged toward a chair.

"Stand still," he said. He lifted the knife, as though to throw it.

And then, behind him, the door opened, and one of the winos stood there, wavering, his shocked eyes taking in the scene.

I said, "It's about time, Lieutenant," and I moved toward the chair as the kid whirled around.

His reaction was fast, I must admit. He turned back

quickly, once he saw who was in the doorway. But I had a chair, by that time, and it was a hefty one. I brought the momentum of my body turn into it and threw low and hard, toward his legs.

One leg caught his knee and he yelped and went crashing backward into the wino. The wino went down and the kid went down with him, half in the saloon, half out on the walk. I picked up another chair and started that way, but the bartender was already over there, a sawed-off axe handle in his hand.

I heard the "thunk" of hickory on skull and the clatter of a knife on the concrete of the walk. I heard a woman scream and the wino curse and the bartender say, "Gosh, I hope to hell I didn't kill him."

I went to the phone as the bartender picked up the knife.

CHAPTER ELEVEN

TRASK SMOKED and ignored me from behind his desk. Caroline came in and said, "Slight concussion. He'll make out."

I asked, "Did you get his prints?"

They ignored me.

I asked, "Did you get the other's kid's prints, the one you picked up earlier?"

Trask looked at me bleakly. "We did. They didn't match."

Caroline said, "Lange's still out there. He claims to be representing this kid, too. He wants him taken to a hospital."

"To hell with Lange," Trask said. "Tell him to talk to Apoyan. I won't talk to the son-of-a-bitch."

Caroline went out, again, and Trask looked at me. He shook his head wearily and looked away.

A thin man in a gray suit came in with some cards and laid them on Trask's desk. "A perfect match. It's the right thumb of that last kid who was brought in."

Dave's dull eyes came to life. "Matches that bloody motel print?"

The thin man nodded. "You'll want them both held?"

"That's right. And tell that shyster out there I've gone to Tibet."

The man went out and Trask looked at me. He half smiled, "Well, that makes you look better to me."

I stood up. "I thought it would. But there's still Nystrom out there, running around loose. I'll go and pick him up for you. Do you want him dead or alive?"

"Just wear a gun," he said. "And don't forget."

It was after five o'clock and I still had an hour or so of paper work ahead of me. I headed back to the office, not looking forward to it.

What does a murder need? Motive, means and opportunity. On the kid, Trask had means; Scott had been killed by a knife and the kid carried a knife. Opportunity, the state would have to prove; that the kid was in the room with the knife when Scott was stabbed. And motive—?

The line would be that the kid worked for Nystrom and Nystrom had been heard threatening Scott.

Why was Trask so happy? Unless the kid confessed, the District Attorney had a long, hard furrow to plough. Trask was banking on the kid's confessing, once the proof of his fingerprint was made clear to him. I had my doubts about the kid confessing to anything.

And there was still Red Nystrom at large, though Trask seemed confident he would be apprehended. I guessed that Trask's current good nature had resulted from the first break he'd had in the case. In my book, he was still a long way from home.

I was halfway through my report for the day when the door opened and Wendell Lange came in. He wasn't looking too worried, but then, it wasn't his neck in danger.

"Bringing me some business?" I asked him.

"I might be. Your friend, Lieutenant Trask, wouldn't talk to me. He's a hard man to reason with, isn't he?"

I stood up and stretched. "I don't know. I guess. What brings you here, Mr. Lange?"

"Certain financial problems. I seem to be dealing with insolvent clients. Murder trials cost money."

"So? A touch? I'm not good for much more than half a buck."

"You represent a wealthy client, though."

"I don't follow you, Mr. Lange."

"She will, I think. She knew Mr. Scott quite well."

I studied him and saw nothing. The tall, thin figure stood there almost casually, the cold blue eyes regarded me impersonally.

I said, "This dialogue is preposterous. Unless there are some things going on that I don't know about."

He expelled his breath audibly. "Things are going on all over town that neither of us know about, Mr. Callahan. In this particular case, I happen to know more of the angles than you do."

"Then take it to the police," I said. "Your concern is with the law, isn't it? That's what you told me this afternoon."

He shook his head. "I told you my first concern was my client. And I intend to buy him all the help that's for sale. That takes more money than he has."

"You want to buy him some witnesses? Which client, Lange?"

"Let's not bicker, Mr. Callahan. I need money. If you want, I'll go directly to your client."

"Do that. And the minute you leave, I'm going to phone the police and tell them about this conversation. Now, get out."

He smiled. "You certainly offer your clients a minimum of protection, don't you? I hope you're not charging them much for that kind of service." He turned, and went out.

I reached for the phone, and paused. I reached for the phone again and got Trask, and lied to him. I said, "Lange was just here. He seems to think he can tap me for money to help with the kid's defense. What in hell would give him that idea?"

"You'd know better than I would, Brock. Come clean."

"So help me, Dave, the guy was talking Greek as far as I'm concerned. It didn't make any kind of sense to me."

"Maybe the shyster's got something on your client, on Mira. He is your client, isn't he?"

"Right from the start. You know that. We were in your office together."

A few seconds of silence, and then, "Your *only* client, Brock?"

"I could hardly run even this small office on one client, Dave. I have another who's going on a retainer as soon as I can draw up the contract."

"I see. You run your office on *two* clients. Who's the other one, Brock?"

I paused and then said, "A local woman, Beverly Hills woman."

"She has a name, I suppose?"

"Miss Glenys Christopher is the name."

"Well—! You're certainly getting the carriage trade, aren't you? What is she, a client or a patron, Callahan?"

"She's a rich and vulnerable girl without any parents in a nasty world." I said. And added the lie. "She's also a Ram fan. So now you know my complete client list to date. And I still can't figure how it would give Lange the idea I'm rich."

Trask chuckled. "Maybe he thinks you're scared. You have reason to be, with Nystrom still at large. Well, we'll check into the Mira angle. And you wear a gun."

I hung up with the untold things still simmering in me. I had told him about Lange's threat and about my two clients. I had given myself an out, but I had given Trask the wrong picture. And that's a lie, slice it how you will. Any words uttered with intent to deceive are lying words, and I had intended to deceive.

I thought back to Dave Trask's office when he'd told me, "But you're in a dirty business, Brock, and you can't stay clean in it, not if you want any new clients."

I reached for the phone again, and drew back again. I remembered Glenys saying, "We need a man, Bobby and I. We need a man I can trust and Bobby can admire."

I didn't pick up the phone again. The telephone company would still be in business tomorrow. I finished the paper work and filed it neatly, and pulled a chair over to the window to watch the traffic.

It was still heavy and I didn't intend to buck it until it thinned out. I wanted to go home and take a long shower and then get drunk and not on beer. I would buy a big bottle of booze and have my semiannual drunk, all alone, at home in Westwood.

The coincidences had screamed at me and I had ignored them, blinded by a pair of long legs and that expensive look. And the promise of a retainer and the unconsciously recognized hope of some payment even beyond that?

Don't muse, Callahan, and don't guess. The phone is staring at you. You are trained to act; leave the thinking to the quarterback.

The phone delivered Glenys Christopher's voice to me and it was a strained voice.

I said, "I want to talk to you, right away. You'll be home, won't you?"

"I'll be home. Has something happened? What's happened? Brock?"

"Lieutenant Trask thinks he has a killer. One of those hot-rod hoodlums has a print that matches one found in the motel room."

"I—heard that. But—I mean, what have I—"

"How did you hear it?" I interrupted her. "Who told you?"

"I—it was on a news report, on the radio or TV. I forget exactly. Brock, what is it? What's wrong?"

"Did Wendell Lange phone you and tell you about the kid? Did he ask for money?"

"Lange—? Brock, you're not making sense."

"Would you answer the question?"

"I don't know any Lange, Brock Callahan."

"All right. Do you want to see me, or don't you?"

A moment's pause, and then, "If you think it's important, I certainly do."

I wasn't hungry. I'd had two luncheons. So I didn't stop for dinner. I locked the office and drove directly to the Christopher's.

Glenys was in pale yellow tonight, her black hair held an orchid. She looked at me humbly, fear in her eyes, standing very quietly in the doorway.

"Shall we go to the patio?" I asked. "I don't want the servants to hear anything."

Interest in the blue eyes, some hope. "All right."

Out there, I sat in one of the cushioned aluminum chairs, she sat on a chaise longue.

I said, "You didn't love Roger Scott, did you? He was just another of your nothings, of your perpetual guests?"

She looked at me without expression. "I think there was a time when I loved him. I wouldn't swear to it, but it seemed like love to me."

"That isn't why you came to me, though. You weren't worried about yourself, or any threat from the killer of Roger Scott."

"What was I worried about?"

"Bobby."

She seemed to flinch. She leaned forward on the chaise longue. "Are you crazy?"

"I might be. Did Bobby know those hoodlums?"

"What hoodlums? Do you mean those two who slashed up your car's upholstery?"

I nodded.

She shook her head. "How could he? Where would he meet boys like that?"

"In Venice. Muscle Beach isn't too far from Venice. Bobby used to go in for that muscle-building mania, didn't he?"

"Yes." For some reason, she seemed relieved, and I wondered if I wasn't off the track.

I hoped I was. I said, "You brought Bobby along the first time you came to my office. Coming to me was his idea, wasn't it?"

"Partially. Brock, you're—"

"Wait," I said. "Maybe my reasons are wrong, but I'm on the right track, despite that. Did Bobby know Rosa Carmona?"

Only the faintest of pauses before she said, "I'm sure he doesn't. Isn't she that dancer?" A strained, false voice.

I nodded and brought out the first lie. "I've a witness who will swear Bobby knew Rosa Carmona."

"If he did, he didn't tell me. What are you trying to say, Brock?"

"I'm not sure, yet. Get Bobby, and we'll ask him."

"He's not home. I don't know where he went."

"Well, try all places you can think of. Did he have dinner already? Won't he be home for dinner?"

"He's had dinner. And I'm not going to disturb a lot of people by phoning them unless you can tell me what's so important about his being here."

"Did you send him away after I phoned you?"

"Brock, what does all this mean? Whom are you working for?"

"I haven't figured that out. You deny that Bobby knew Rosa Carmona or the hoodlums?"

"I only deny that I know about it, if it's true. I doubt it very much. And if he did, what does that prove?"

"That's what I hoped you would tell me. You came into my office right after you read about Scott's death. A shyster lawyer named Wendell Lange today implied that you'd pay him money. This lawyer represents the hoodlums and Red Nystrom. I can't see that you would be implicated, but you admitted to me that there are times when Bobby's arrogant. Bobby is your responsibility and I think you feel that very strongly. I thought for a while, there, that you were jealous of Jan Bonnet. Wasn't that egotistical of me? You were only worried that she would tell me about Bobby and Rosa Carmona. She's close enough to Bobby to know about that, isn't she?"

Glenys said hoarsely, "She's your witness? She's the one who told you about Bobby and this Carmona person?"

I shook my head. "Not a word. My witness is from the other end of town."

"That—girl who was killed, that Sue Ellen?"

I shook my head again.

Glenys rubbed the back of one hand across her forehead. "Brock, you haven't taken this ridiculous story to the police, have you?"

"If it's ridiculous, it shouldn't bother you."

"Won't it? Can't you see the papers? Does it matter to them whether it's true or not? And Bobby just starting college. Haven't you any sense of—of—" She broke off and tears began to run down her cheeks. "You—you— monster—" She put her head forward into her hands.

"Did Lange phone you?" I asked her gently.

"Go away," she said chokingly. "Please get out of here, Brock."

"I'm still working for you, Glenys," I said softly. "I'm still on your side. But I've got to have the truth."

"Truth—?" She looked up. "You come here and accuse Bobby of God knows what—and *then* ask for the truth?"

"Did Lange phone you?" I asked for the third time.

"Some lawyer phoned me. Yes, I believe his name was Lange. He phoned a little while before you did. And he didn't threaten me, either."

"But he asked for money."

"He said he knew I was interested in finding the real killer of Roger Scott. And he said the real killer would never be found if some innocent lad was railroaded to the gas chamber for the murder. He thought I should be interested in saving an innocent young man."

"And how much would that cost?"

"Five thousand dollars, to start with. He said he might have to make further demands on me later."

"Blackmail," I said. "He can weasel-word it any way he wants, but it's still blackmail."

She looked at me candidly and nodded. "I suppose it is. I'd pay a lot more than that to—to—"

"Save Bobby?" I finished for her.

"Do you think Bobby's a—a killer?"

"It's hard to believe," I said. "In the heat of anger, or the influence of alcohol, anyone could be a killer, I suppose."

"Bobby doesn't drink."

"No. But he loves his sister. And if he should learn that some filthy angle-shooter she was infatuated with was really a pornographic picture peddler, he might—"

She shook her head. "No. There's nothing there, *nothing*."

"I might still be right, though for the wrong reasons," I said. "Bobby is involved in all this that has happened, isn't he?"

"You're blundering around in the dark," she said quietly.

"I don't know what your purposes are, but you don't really know anything, do you? But you concocted this absurd thesis and thought you could bring it up here and scare me with it. Why, Brock?"

I didn't answer.

"For money, Brock?"

I stood up. "I guess we're getting nowhere, Glenys. There's no faith between us. I hope, when Bobby comes home, he'll have more faith—and more sense. Tell him I was here, won't you? And why?"

Then, from the entrance to the living room, a voice said, "I'm here, Brock. I've been here all along."

CHAPTER TWELVE

GLENYS SAID quickly, "Bobby, you—fool! He's not on our side. He hasn't the faintest idea about any of it. He's trying to blackmail us."

I looked at Bobby and Bobby looked at me. His smile was weak, but it was a smile. "Not Brock," he said quietly. "Not the Rock. You couldn't be more wrong on him, Sis."

"Thanks, Bobby," I said. "Do you want to give me the story?"

He nodded. "Here? Or at the station?"

"Right here," I said. "Just the three of us. *And all of it, Bobby.*"

He sat down next to his sister on the chaise longue. He leaned forward with his elbows on his knees and his fingers laced. I'd seen a lot of players sit like that in the locker room, before a big game.

He said, "I know Rosa Carmona. I was in love with her. That's real crazy, huh?"

"I don't know," I said. "I never met her."

"Great party girl," Bobby said. "No—pushover, but she did—I mean, she said it was because it was love. Are you with me?"

I nodded.

"It gets funnier," Bobby went on. "I wanted to marry her. Maybe it's—because I didn't have much experience with girls like that. Anyway, I wanted to marry her. I was real hot for marrying her. Why aren't you laughing, Brock?"

"Maybe it isn't funny," I answered.

"Sure. Maybe. I don't know." He shook his head and looked at the concrete of the patio. "Then Jan told me the girl was a tramp."

"You'd never guessed that?" I asked.

"I figured she had been. I figured we had something a little better than that. Golly, she was fun. I mean—well, happiness just seemed to surround her."

"Where'd you meet her, Bobby?"

"At that bar in Venice, that place where the blonde got shotgunned."

"Uh-huh. So Jan told you she was a tramp. Then what?"

"So I got mad at Jan. I wouldn't take any nasty talk, not about Rosa, not from *anybody*." He shook his head slowly.

Glenys reached over to put a hand on his shoulder.

"And then?" I asked.

"And then Jan said she'd prove it to me, that the girl was a tramp, right then, and sleeping with Roger Scott. She told me about the motel, and told me how to get to Scott's room that back way."

"And you went over there?"

He nodded. "I had a couple drinks, first. I never drink, Brock, not since the first time I tried it, when I was sixteen. I don't drink. I stay in shape, Brock."

I smiled at him. "Okay, you stay in shape. There are more important things to think about right now. Go on."

"I had a couple drinks, or I never would have gone over there. I believed in the girl, Brock."

I nodded. "Go on."

"It gets kind of mixed up, now," he said. "So help me, I can't be sure of what happened, exactly." He looked at Glenys, and at me, and back at the concrete. "I had a key. They were there, all right, Scott and Rosa. And Rosa without a damned stitch on."

I asked quietly. "You had a key? Who gave it to you?"

He said hoarsely, "Jan."

"Go on," I said.

"I don't know. I was mad and drunk and sick. I remember I hit him. I hit him clean and hard a couple times. And he was on the floor and he didn't get up. I remember that damned well."

"Were you carrying a knife, Bobby?"

He stared at me. "A knife? What am I? You know I wouldn't have anything to do with a knife, Brock."

"All right. Go on."

Rosa started to give me the business. Said he'd told her he was an artist and wanted to paint her, and then when she got there he'd made improper advances. Man, she must have thought I was some square, huh?"

"She had reason to," I said. "Go on."

He looked at his hands. "I hit her. I'm not proud of it. I hit her. And I called her a—I called her some nasty names. I hit her and got out of there. I don't even remember driving home." He stared at his hands, flexing and unflexing them.

Glenys said quietly, "And the next morning we came to you." She paused. "For help."

I looked at her evenly. "And lied to me."

She nodded. "If it was your brother, would you have lied?"

I didn't answer. I asked Bobby, "Don't you remember anything more about that night? Were there any other cars you might have noticed on that street?"

He frowned and rubbed one wrist with the heel of the other hand. "Let's see—"

Glenys asked quietly, "Like a mustard-colored Chev, do you mean, Brock?"

"No, I don't mean a Chev. Was there one there, Bobby?"

He shook his head stubbornly. "Wait—there was a rod, but I figured it was for one of the houses on that side street. It was a '33 or '34 Ford."

"A coupe, chopped and channeled?"

He nodded quickly. "That's right, a black one. Does that mean something, Brock?"

"It could. When was the last time you saw Rosa, Bobby?"

"That was the last time."

"Dead or alive, the last time?"

He looked up quickly. "Dead—? Rosa's dead? Hell, she couldn't— Tell me, Brock, is she dead?"

I shrugged. "Nobody seems to know."

He shook his head. "I can't think of her dead. She was too—too alive."

"Everybody dies," I said, "even the live ones." I stood up for the second time. "There's nothing more, Bobby? That's it?"

He looked at me anxiously. "That's it, Brock. Are you going to the police now?"

"No, not now. I work with the police, but *for* the Christophers. I'll keep in touch with you." I looked at Glenys. "Don't pay anything to Lange. I'll try and get in touch with him tonight."

"Thank you, Brock," Glenys said.

I asked her, "Why did you originally come to me? Because you wanted to get me off the other investigation? Or did you think you could buy me?"

She shook her head slowly. "Not *buy* you, rent you. I needed a friend, and I'm used to paying for my friends."

Neither of them got up; I went to the door alone and out into a cool dusk. The sprinklers were throwing a mist over the immense lawns that sloped away from the house on all sides.

I thought of the girl Bobby had brought to the party and wondered at his love for Rosa Carmona. This Rosa must have something to compete successfully with dolls like Bobby's Dianne. The chances were she had one appeal very few men can resist—she was available.

I decided to eat in Hollywood and my route took me past Lange's office. I parked and went up.

The girl with the scrubbed face looked at me coolly. "Mr. Lange isn't in. Is there a message?"

"None. You're working late, aren't you? Is he coming back?"

"He didn't say. I doubt it. He very rarely works after six."

"Could you phone him at home and ask him if he would talk to me there?"

"I could. What is the nature of the business, Mr. Callahan?"

"An attempt at blackmail on his part."

She looked at me quietly.

"Adjust," I told her. "You're in Hollywood."

She picked up the phone on her desk and dialed a number. A moment, and she said, "Mr. Callahan is here, Mr. Lange. He'd like to talk to you tonight."

Another moment, and she handed me the phone.

Lange said, "I'm just eating dinner, Mr. Callahan. Could you make it eight-thirty, here at my home?"

"I'll be there," I said, and hung up.

The girl wrote an address on a slip of paper and handed it to me. She avoided my eyes.

"We all have to eat," I told her.

I ate dinner at *The Shorthorn* in Hollywood and then sent the flivver up one of the winding roads that led into Hollywood Hills.

The home of Wendell Lange had probably been constructed before real estate went crazy out here. It was a solid place, though not too big, buried in geraniums behind a white-washed split-rail fence.

Wendell Lange was waiting for me in the small front patio. I could see through the living room windows behind him. I could see an attractive middle-aged woman reading a storybook to a pair of girls just short of their teens. They looked like twins.

Lange got up from the wicker chair he'd been sitting in. It was dark now, but I could see his face reflected in the glow from the living room. He was smoking a cigar that smelled expensive.

"Twins?" I asked him.

"What—?" He paused. "Oh." He turned to look back into the lighted living room. "Twins. Pretty, aren't they?"

"In a few years, they'll be dating, I'll bet." My voice was weary. "Let's hope they don't get a yen for any hot-rodders."

He said nothing.

"Nice place, you have," I said. I turned to look at the lighted city below us. "Some view."

He nodded. "I could sell it for four times what I paid for it. I hope you didn't come here to lecture me, Mr. Callahan." He indicated another wicker chair. "Won't you sit down?"

I sat down. "Nystrom ever been here?" I asked.

"Stop it, Mr. Callahan. We all play the roles we choose. If I want a lecture on the moralities, I can find a lecturer better equipped and educated than you."

"Okay, Mr. Lange, I'll be blunt. The police can't seem to understand why I've refused to positively identify Red Nystrom as the killer of Sue Ellen. I can't quite understand it, myself. I suppose I'm splitting hairs."

His back was to the light and I couldn't see his face now. He said, "Are you offering me some kind of trade, Mr. Callahan?"

"I'm stating some facts. Here's another—my client

doesn't care to pay me any more to find the murderer of Roger Scott. She's satisfied with the suspect the police are holding."

"I guess the police are, too. There was another boy there, that night, wasn't there?"

"Possibly. But anyone who claimed that would also be admitting that he was there. And it would be wise for him to have a *reason* for being there."

"I see your point. Go on, Mr. Callahan."

"There might have been a girl there, too. I've been hired to find her, a girl named Rosa Carmona. Do you know where she is?"

"I don't."

"Does Red? Couldn't you ask him?"

"Red Nystrom? I suppose, if I knew where he was, I could ask him."

"You don't know where Red is?"

A long pause, and then, "I don't."

"Nor Rosa Carmona?"

"I don't." Another pause. "And I've a strange feeling Mr. Nystrom doesn't know, either. Though that's just a guess, of course."

"Of course. But if there were two boys and Scott and Rosa in that motel room that night, we have available as witnesses only the two boys, haven't we?"

"Would you care to name the two boys? We seem to be dealing with a lot of—theoretical people here."

"One of the boys is the lad the police are holding. The other could be his buddy or it could be one of my clients. Or maybe even both. At any rate, you're representing some pretty vicious people. And you expect an innocent person to help pay for the defense of these—"

"*Poorer* people," he supplied for me. "I'm not interested in your evaluation of their characters. You took a very roundabout way of saying 'no,' Mr. Callahan. Your client doesn't intend to contribute to the defense of this lad?"

"Not if I have anything to say about it," I told him.

"I see. And you're threatening me with a change of testimony regarding Red Nystrom if I don't play ball."

"That's putting it kind of bluntly. I wonder if Red shouldn't be consulted. He'd be unhappy, I'll bet, if he found out you had changed my testimony by your lack of cooperation. Red might not understand that." I looked past him, through the living room windows.

"Don't," he said. "I've been practicing a long time, Mr. Callahan. I'm safe from any criminal threat, I assure you."

"From any *intelligent* criminal threat," I corrected him. "Nobody in the world, including Red's mother, is safe from a man like Red Nystrom."

"That needn't be your concern. What you've almost told me, Callahan, is that you'd perjure yourself if I didn't stay away from Miss Christopher."

"No. I'm simply asking that you be ethical because we're being ethical." I stood up. "I don't seem to get anywhere with you. If you see Red, tell him I'm still waiting for that meeting."

He nodded. "If I see him, I'll be sure to tell him that." He stood up. "And if you don't mind some advice from an old pro, Mr. Callahan, get into another line of work. You're entirely too naive for this business."

"There should be room for one honest man in it," I said. "I think your wife is trying to get your attention."

He looked at the window, where his wife was outlined. "Yes," he said quietly, "it's time to hear the children's prayers. Good night, Mr. Callahan."

I drove down the hill again, thinking of Jan, wondering if she'd be home. And I thought about Bobby and wondered how true his story was. He's given it to me earnestly and apparently honestly, but he'd looked just as honest when he first came to me.

Jan and Bobby I wanted to believe in, which is the wrong approach. *Be objective, Callahan, not sentimental.* Glenys, for all her beauty, had rarely got through to me; I had no sense of empathy with her. Glenys. though, was less involved in this mess than either Jan or Bobby. At least, that's the way it seemed.

And where was Rosa Carmona?

The flivver threw out big clouds of unignited exhaust gasses as we came to the bottom of the hill. I turned right on Sunset, heading for Beverly Glen, framing soft words in my mind.

I thought of Bobby's talk with me in the office when he'd said of his sister, "She sails for you, Brock."

Was the kid a pathological liar or was he using all the weapons he could find to keep me on his side? And now, this latest story—how could I judge its truth?

There was a light in the window of the Bonnet cottage. The dog next door started to bark as I came up her stepping stones toward the light.

She was wearing a robe, and her hair was up in curlers and there was cream on her face. She still looked good.

"Hmmmm," she said. "Now what—?"

"I like your hair straight," I told her. "Why are you curling it?"

"No small talk, Brock. I can tell by your face that you're here for a purpose."

"Bobby Christopher has just told me an amazing story," I said. "May I come in?"

She looked at me, wide-eyed. Then, she nodded, and stood aside for me to enter.

I smelled coffee and cosmetics. I said, "I could use some coffee. I've a headache."

"I'll bring some. It's still hot." She went into the kitchen and I sat on a circular couch in the corner with a triangular coffee table in front of it.

From the kitchen, she called, "Cream? Sugar?"

"Neither," I answered.

When she came back into the living room, the cream was off her face. She set the cup of coffee on the table in front of me. "I hope you like it strong."

"I do tonight. Jan—how much do you know about Bobby and Rosa Carmona?"

She sat near me, on the end of the couch, half turned to face me. "I knew he wanted to marry her."

"And that she was—a friend of Scott's?"

She inhaled heavily and seemed to hold her breath. "Yes. That's when I learned what Roger Scott really was."

I said nothing.

"He met Rosa through Bobby," Jan went on. "Bobby was proud of her, you see. He even had her up to his house for dinner."

I said nothing.

Jan said softly, "All right, blow up. I lied to you didn't I?"

"You're not the only one. You still had the key to Scott's place. And you'd learned about Rosa. So you gave the key to Bobby so he could learn about Rosa. But still you went to Scott's funeral."

"Why not?"

"After learning what he was—and remembering what you two had been, you could still mourn him?"

"He was dead. He'd been a friend. I can't hate the dead."

"All right. And you were silent about the rest of it because you wanted to protect the Christophers?"

"*Bobby* Christopher. He's a fine kid, Brock. And you know he's no killer."

"Nobody can be sure," I answered. "Killers come in all weights and sizes and qualities."

"But kids like Bobby don't carry knives."

"I wasn't thinking of Roger Scott."

"Who then? That woman in Venice, the one who was killed with a shotgun?"

I shook my head. "I was thinking of Rosa Carmona."

"Is she dead, too? When did this—"

"I don't know if she's dead," I interrupted. Though it seems very likely. But if she isn't dead, where the hell is she?"

"I've no idea, Brock. Would you like some aspirin?"

"No, the coffee will do it. Jan, if there's anything that will help, tell me, won't you? I didn't come here to question your motives or your morals. I'm looking for a girl."

She told me all of her part in it and it matched Bobby's story. She finished with, "That's probably why Glenys was so frightened by your interest in me." She smiled. "I suppose you thought she was jealous."

"Bobby tried to convince me she was, but I'm not quite that egotistical. And besides, that Glenys is a pretty cool dish of tea. I've a feeling men aren't too important to her."

"You're wrong on that. They are."

Next door, the dog started to bark again. I finished my coffee and looked at the headline on the late edition of the *Examiner*.

Teen-ager Held In Motel Killing. it read, There was a picture of the kid who'd come for me with a knife. There was a picture of his buddy, and his buddy's mother sitting on a bench. She was crying, her head bent forward in shame.

I said, "I wonder if Bobby knew those kids. He's been in that saloon where they hang around."

"I don't think he knew them. Brock, are you going to tell the police about Bobby?"

I rubbed my forehead. "I don't know. There's a shyster lawyer who knows he was there that night, too. He might tell them, just to confuse the case as much as possible."

"You need some aspirin," she said. "Why are you being stubborn about it?" She stood up and went to the bathroom.

When she came back, she had a bottle of aspirin and a glass of water. I took two of them and thanked her, and stood up.

"You look tired," she said.

"I am. One more call and it's the hay for me."

She came with me to the door. There, she put a hand on my arm. "I'm sorry I lied to you, Brock. It didn't do any good, anyway, did it?"

I leaned over and kissed her on the forehead. "You were loyal—and sentimental. That's no crime—yet. I'll be seeing you."

There was no sound from the dog as I went down the stepping stones to my car. I cut back to Wilshire and took that to San Vicente and San Vicente to Brentwood.

Randall came out, the registry card in his hand, as I pulled the flivver into his parking area. Then he saw I was alone in the car, and waited in the doorway. Only the couples got curb service here, probably.

He sighed when he recognized me. "The police have been here, and now you. They nailed that young hoodlum, I see."

"They've picked him up, but he's a long way from nailed. Had you ever seen him around here?"

"Never. I had a feeling that Sergeant Pascal wanted me to say I had."

"I guess the police still don't trust you, Mr. Randall."

"They don't trust anybody. I don't see anything in the papers about them picking up Red Nystrom."

"It's only a question of time, I've been told."

I went into the narrow office, and he closed the door behind us. He looked at me doubtfully.

I said, "I've just been talking to Red's lawyer. He seems to think there was somebody else the police don't know about who was here that night. It must have been a regular convention."

He said nothing.

"That many people would cause a stir," I went on. "I'm surprised you didn't hear something."

"Every unit has a radio and a TV set," he answered. "At times, it sounds like a blacksmith shop around here, despite the thick walls in this place."

"I can see why you'd be suspicious of the police," I continued. "But my client isn't close to the police."

He looked at me guardedly. "What are you trying to say, Mr. Callahan?"

"I thought you might tell me something you wouldn't tell them."

"I already got hell from the police for telling you about that fingerprint."

"If you hadn't told me that, they wouldn't have this punk locked up now. I'm the one who suggested they check him. As a matter of fact, I'm the one who brought him in. That's gratitude for you, isn't it?"

"I don't know what it is. This I know, the police have my whole story and it's the only one I have and if you want it, you can ask them for it."

"You've got a short memory," I told him. "Remember

the day Red walked in here and told me to leave? And I didn't, did I? I stuck by you, then, didn't I?"

"You stuck. And I hit him with a chair. And now he's out there, somewhere, free and operating. And I can't sleep nights. Mr. Callahan, I've said all I'm going to. Good night."

"Good night," I said. And added the Bonnet line. "Good luck."

CHAPTER THIRTEEN

Two corpses, two killers; what did I want? The police were happy. Why shouldn't I be? For one thing, I'd been hired to find Rosa Carmona, and I hadn't found her. For another thing, Bobby Christopher was involved in the mess and I had accepted the Christophers as clients.

The headache was mostly gone, but my bones ached as I steered the flivver back to Westwood. My knee twinged as I swung my right foot from the accelerator to the brake for the light on Wilshire.

Maybe the kid Trask was holding wasn't the killer. The fingerprint would establish his being in the room and with blood on his hand, but could they establish it was Scott's blood?

Well, Trask was happy and he knew more about those things than I did. But Trask didn't know about Bobby Christopher, not yet. *Are you going to tell him, Callahan?*

The light changed and I cut into the stream of Wilshire traffic. On Westwood, I turned off and took that half a block to the alley that served the garages.

I remember reading a piece by Irvin S. Cobb once where he stated that driving into a battle area in the First World War had given him a strange feeling of being on a stage where everybody was watching. Because the attention of the world was centered on that particular area.

Driving up that alley, I got goose pimples for no reason I could analyze at the time. I had a feeling of someone's—*presence* in the area, some evil and violent aura that seemed to hang in the damp night air.

Nerves, I told myself. *You're tired and sick, Callahan; you're seeing ghosts.*

My garage door was open. The lights of the flivver illuminated the interior of the garage and there was nothing there, nothing that shouldn't be.

I drove in, and turned off the lights and sat for a second, listening for a sound. There was none. I climbed out, and the interior lights went on briefly and went out as I closed the door of the car. The sound of the door's closing seemed to echo in the other garages.

I took three steps, and was reaching up for the overhead door, to close it, when a voice said, "Hello, Callahan."

From the shrubbery on the other side of the alley, I saw a figure silhouetted. It was a broad-shouldered figure, but I couldn't see the face; the dim light from a house was behind him.

"Red—?" I asked.

"That's right, Callahan. And I've got a gun in my hand."

"I talked with your lawyer tonight, Red." Sweat ran down my sides, and there was a bitter, bile-like taste in my mouth.

"Threatening to change your testimony, I hear."

I thought of Wendell Lange and started to speak. I thought of his daughters, and closed my mouth.

Red's voice was taunting. "You scared speechless, Callahan? Kids are your meat, aren't they, punks with knives?"

"I'm scared," I admitted. "You play it too heavy, Red. You could be sitting high right now, if you'd use your head instead of your muscles."

"Close the door, like you were going to," he said. "Then go up the back way to your apartment. I'll be right behind you."

Dave Trask had told me to carry a gun. How stupid I had been. First the hot-rodder with a knife and now Red with a gun. Lange had worded it, I was too naive for this business. I reached up again and pulled the garage door down. I kept my hand on it all the way, so it wouldn't bang at the bottom.

Red chuckled. "Footballer—Aren't you a prize? Big, tough footballer, scared silly."

"You've got a gun," I said. "I haven't."

"And I've got friends with guns," he said. "And knives and brass knuckles and all the guts they need. So don't get any cute ideas, Callahan. Just walk ahead of me a few steps, easy and slow."

I walked ahead of him, not knowing when his gun would go off. But if he'd meant to shoot me outside, he would have done it in the alley. I kept telling myself.

But if it was just talk he wanted, he could have talked in the alley, too. The bitter taste was still in my mouth. At the back gate to the court, I paused.

I said quietly, "I've only one door to my apartment, and we have to go through the court to get to it. Somebody might still be sitting up in the court."

"Go ahead," he said. "The gun's in my pocket."

There was nobody in the court. We walked through, past the fountain, to the iron steps. Going up, I considered my chances of getting away, of backing up and perhaps catching him unprepared. They were narrow steps and if he was close enough, I might be able to topple him backwards.

He said, "Don't get any ideas, Callahan. This is an easy trigger."

I killed the ideas I'd been considering and walked along the narrow iron walk to my door. I had some trouble with the key; my hand was trembling. But I managed it, finally, and opened the door.

Then I paused and asked quietly, "Do you want the light on?"

"Right."

I reached around the open doorway and found the light switch and snapped it. The table lamp near the windows went on.

Red said, "Go over and close those shades."

I went over and pulled down the shades while he waited in the doorway. Then he came in and locked the door behind him.

"Sit down," he said.

I sat in a pull-up chair as he turned. I could see the gun in his hand, now, and it looked like a service .45 to me. They make a big hole.

He had some surgical dressing on his head, a reminder of Randall's chair. He still had the black eye and puffed nose, a reminder of Callahan's knee.

"Put your hands on the arms of the chair," he said.

I did.

He came over to stand within slugging distance, the hole in the end of the .45 looking like a tunnel, this close.

His smile was anticipatory. "I told you we'd meet again."

"I was hoping it wouldn't be this soon," I said.

"Getting gutty, huh? You're not even trembling much, any more."

I said nothing.

"What's Trask got?" he asked. "What's he so damned happy about?"

"I don't know, Red. I've been trying to figure that one, too."

"Don't give me that, footballer. He's got Rosa, hasn't he?"

I shook my head.

The back of his left hand came swinging like the boom of a sailing ship. It caught me on the cheek and the chair tilted over on two legs for a second and I could feel blood running.

For a moment, I almost lost control. I half rose from the chair.

The hole in the .45 came up to stare into my left eye, and I settled back again. I put a hand to my cheek and it came away smeared with blood.

"You could take off the ring," I said.

"You could live, too," he said. "Just tell me where Rosa is. You've got some lumps coming, Callahan, but I didn't come here to kill you. Not unless I have to."

"You tell me about Rosa," I said. "Maybe I can guess where she is from that."

"I'll ask you again," he said. "Where's Rosa?"

My head was still ringing from his last slap. And I knew he could kill without thinking. I tried to dream up a lie, but my brain was a shambles.

"I don't know," I said. "I honestly don't know."

I felt the cutting edges of the diamond across the bridge of my nose, this time, and the pain of exposed bone needled my brain.

"Damn it, Red," I said sickly, "I'm getting paid to find her. And I haven't. I want to know as badly as you do. I'm your best witness, Red; you're cutting your own throat."

He took a step backward, the gun steady in his hand, studying me thoughtfully.

I don't know what made me think of it; probably the way he'd taken that backward step. Like a place kicker. I'd done a lot of place kicking at Stanford, but very little with the Rams. And never with my left foot.

But the gun was in line with my left leg, now, and the distance was right. If I could catch him with the edge of my shoe's sole, catch him cleanly on the wrist bone; there was a fifty-fifty chance he would drop the gun.

His eyes were shining and his voice was tight. "Once more, Callahan. Where's Rosa?"

"The last time I saw her," I began slowly—and put a hand to my cheek. I wanted his gaze high. "The last time I saw her, she—"

I swung the left leg up sharply, and ducked to the right. I felt the impact and heard the clatter of the gun on the thin carpet on the floor.

And then Red made his big mistake. He could have handled me with his hands, I felt sure. He'd proved that at the motel. He'd done a lot more fighting than I had.

But he went down for the gun, stooping for it. And that put him into a position roughly resembling an opposing lineman. In that position, he was no less vulnerable than lovable Ed Sprinkle.

I caught him right behind the ear with my right hand and flush in the teeth with my right knee. He went over sideways, and for a moment he was on his back. I dropped on him, both knees to the groin, and reached out my left hand to get a firm grip on his Adam's apple.

My first punch to the button with my right hand did it. If it hadn't, I would have torn his throat out with my left.

There was a babble of voices in the hall as I went over to pick up the gun. Someone knocked on my door.

I opened it to face Paul Kimball. I said, "Call the police, Paul. Right from here."

I checked the gun to be sure there was a cartridge in the chamber and went over to stand close to Red.

"Your face, Brock," Paul said. "It's streaming blood."

"I know. Phone, phone, phone—*Hurry, man!*"

Captain Apoyan's office was neat and small and orderly, like Captain Apoyan. He was a fairly short man, and slim for an Armenian, with big brown eyes that were never quiet.

He said, "I've sent for Doctor Ritter, Brock. You won't have a scar, I'll bet, when he gets through. Those bandages are only temporary."

"I'm not sure I can afford Doctor Ritter," I said. "I'm not sure my face is that important."

"You can afford the Department rate for Ritter. I've put Red in a cell across from that kid. I want the kid to see that face. The boys made a lot of noise going down, and turned on some lights. The kid will wake up and see his hero; we'll see to that."

"Is it smart to put them close enough so they can talk things over?"

"There'll be a man listening, don't worry. The kid's old man brought a priest in, and even that didn't touch him." Apoyan shook his head. "God, those punks can be stubborn."

"They're not old enough to know about deals, yet," I said.

Apoyan looked at me suspiciously. Then he reached over to pick up a package of cigarettes from his desk. He offered me one.

I shook my head. "I don't smoke."

Apoyan smiled. "Figure you can make it in the Canadian League, or something?"

I didn't answer. My headache was back and the pain in my nose seemed to throb with the beat of my heart.

"I sent for Trask," Apoyan said. "He's more familiar with this case than I am. You can give him the story of it. Want to lie down, Brock?" He nodded toward a couch against one wall.

I rose. "I think I will. And could I have a big glass of cold water? And maybe some aspirin?"

"Of course you can," he said gently. "Go and lie down, Brock. Leave everything to me."

A uniformed man stuck his head through the doorway. "Attorney Wendell Lange is waiting to talk with you, Captain."

"Let him sit a while. Get my boy here some cold water and a couple aspirin tablets, officer."

"Yes, sir," the man said, and went away.

"Could you open a window?" I asked. "I'm getting sick."

"Reaction," Apoyan said soothingly. "It happens that way. Try not to think of it, Brock." He went over to open a window.

I had my aspirin and my cold water. I even had my wrists bathed with cool, wet cloths. And then Trask came.

And the atmosphere changed.

I gave him my story and saw no compassion on his face. When I'd finished, he said, "Where is this Rosa?"

"I've no idea, so help me, Dave."

Trask looked at me coldly. "There are things you know you're not telling me. I suppose you think you have a friend at court in Captain Apoyan? We know about Glenys Christopher being your client."

"I don't want to argue with you, Dave. I want to phone my lawyer."

"Go ahead. You'll need him." He got up and went out.

Doctor Ritter came and patched me up and Tommy Self came after the doctor had finished.

Tommy had been a fine Stanford quarterback and he'd had some Harvard after that. He was my attorney.

I told him, "I want you to get in touch with a client of mine, a Miss Glenys Christopher. I want you to tell her that I was working on the Scott case for her because Scott owed her ten thousand dollars when he died. That is absolutely all she is to tell the police. She is to bring an attorney along if they try to bring her down here. I want you to phone her and tell her that the second you leave."

Tommy frowned at me. "Brock, I'm not like that slob out there, that Lange. I'm ethical, Brock."

"Who said you weren't?"

"You gave me a message. I'm no courier; I'm an attorney. And it sounded like a phoney message to me. I can't buck the law, Brock."

"Not even to save the rep of a very promising quarterback?"

He stared at me. "Are you punchy?" And then, slowly, "Christopher—? Did you say Christopher?"

"That's what I said."

"And you want me to *sneak* a message out, just to—"

"Save it, you card shark," I interrupted. "Where the hell did you suddenly pick up all these ethics? Did Harvard do that to you?"

"Bobby Christopher—" Self said quietly, and shook his head. "Hey, didn't he sign up for S.C.?"

"Not yet," I lied. "Maybe we can still swing him."

Tommy shook his head and his gaze moved around my bandaged face. "You were always an honest man," he said softly.

"I still am, Tommy. Get moving. Go."

He nodded. "Yup. Okay, Brock. For you."

He went out and I went back to the couch to lie down. A uniformed man came in and pulled a chair over near the doorway and sat down on it.

I closed my eyes and tried to find some mental stability. I stretched my back, arching it. I asked the uniformed man, "Would you take off my shoes?"

He looked at me hesitantly, and then shrugged. He came over to unlace and pull off my shoes.

It didn't seem logical that I would fall asleep, with all the angles I had prodding me. But I did fall asleep, and I dreamed.

I dreamed Bobby was working out of the T, and going back to pass, fading, fading, fading, looking for a receiver.

Then, finally, way down field a man broke loose from his defender and reached his long arms up as Bobby arched a sixty yarder. The man had turned to take the pass and I could see his face.

It was Red Nystrom.

CHAPTER FOURTEEN

SOMEBODY WAS shaking me and I wakened. The room was dimmer, only Captain Apoyan's desk lamp was now lighted. The uniformed officer over me said, "Trask wants to see you in his office. Need any help?"

"No, I'm all right." I rose to a sitting position and my brain seemed to rattle. I took a deep breath.

"Easy does it," the uniformed man said. "Wait'll I get your shoes on."

As he put them on, I asked, "Who's in there?"

"Your attorney. And some girl. Tall girl, with black hair. Looks like a rich girl to me. Sergeant Pascal's in there, too."

"Didn't the girl bring her attorney?"

"No. I guess your attorney's representing her. Can you make it all right?"

"Lead the way," I said.

We went down the hall to Trask's office. The officer stepped aside for me to enter, and I went in. He closed the door behind me, from the other side.

Glenys Christopher's eyes went to my bandaged face, and she gasped. "Brock, what happened—?"

"Haven't you been told?"

I thought Tommy Self looked uncomfortable. Pascal nodded toward a chair near Dave Trask's desk, and I sat down.

Dave said, "I've been up since seven in the morning and it's now three o'clock. We'll save a lot of time if the two of you tell me all you know about Roger Scott's death."

"You should have gone to bed, Dave," I said. "I've

already told you all I know. If you want me to, I can bring you the rest of my reports tomorrow."

Trask looked from me to Glenys. "Would you tell me, Miss Christopher, just what your relationship was with Roger Scott?"

She gave him the Beverly Hills freeze. "I don't understand the question, Sergeant Trask."

He smiled. "*Lieutenant* Trask, Miss Christopher. I mean, you lent him ten thousand dollars. Why?"

"Because he asked for it. I certainly didn't volunteer it."

"I see. He was a friend of yours, then?"

She shrugged. "Not too good a friend. He wanted twenty thousand dollars."

I chuckled, and Pascal looked at me coldly. Nobody else seemed to think it was funny.

Trask said, "You won't admit you were in love with him?"

"I won't deny it. I don't remember the state of my affections when we were seeing the most of each other. He wasn't really in my—set, you know. My friends never accepted him. As a matter of fact, I remember Elsbeth MacDonald telling me one time that she thought he was a fortune hunter. But of course, Elsbeth—"

I had to hand it to her. Earlier this evening, she'd been in a state of shock, almost. And now she was putting it on as thick as a starlet at a producer's party.

Trask cut in with, "You paid him by check?"

"I don't remember. I told my business manager to pay him, but I don't remember if he told me how he was paid."

"Your business manager is available now, is he? Could you have him come in tomorrow?"

"I doubt it. He's off the coast of Spain, somewhere, one of those islands—is it Majorca? Or is that off Florida? Is that one of the Keys? I mean, I—"

"He has an office, hasn't he? The records will be available in his office, won't they?"

"I suppose. Is it so important, Lieutenant? Do you think I'm lying to you?"

Trask looked at Pascal and sighed. Self looked at me and shrugged. Glenys covered a yawn, and asked, "Exactly why did you want to see me, Lieutenant? If it's about Roger Scott's death, I was giving a rather large party that night. I hope you don't think I killed Mr. Scott? Because if you do, I can bring in any number of witnesses as to my whereabouts that evening. Including the Governor. Would you mind coming to the point?"

Trask said patiently, "We want to know why you contracted for the services of Mr. Callahan, Miss Christopher. And I'd appreciate a short and straight answer."

"Because I wanted to find out who killed Roger, for one thing. And I wanted to learn how much chance I had of getting my money back. I expected Mr. Callahan would investigate both."

"And why Mr. Callahan?"

"Because he's in Beverly Hills and I happened to be in the neighborhood, shopping, that morning."

"I see. And how long has Mr. Self been your attorney?"

"He isn't my attorney. He's only representing me at the moment. My regular attorney was lost to me when he was elected Governor of this state and I haven't replaced him, as yet."

Trask took a big, deep breath, like a man going down into deep water. "And why were you interested in who killed Roger Scott?"

"I wasn't really interested in who killed him; I just wanted to make sure it wasn't one of my friends. I certainly didn't want to have any corpses turn up at one of my parties."

Trask looked at me and back at Glenys. "Miss Christopher, you may think me fool enough to be taken in by this ridiculous dialogue. Or you might think me small enough to be impressed by your social position. I'm neither, and I'd appreciate some straight talk."

Glenys looked at him coolly and patronizingly. "I've talked as honestly and completely as I could, Lieutenant. You may address any further questions to Mr. Self."

Dave looked at me. "And you, Callahan?"

"I'm sick of doing your work, Dave, and I'm physically sick, too. To hell with you and your idiot employees."

Tommy said, "Easy, Brock. There's no point in being abusive. The Lieutenant's only trying to get at the truth."

"You don't know him, Tommy," I said. "He's lied to me from the first day I was brought in here. I'm getting sick of the smell of this place. I've cooperated 200 per cent with the whole lying bunch of them right from that first day. And now he can do any damned thing with me he wants. I've got a story the papers will love, and they're getting it."

Trask looked at me bleakly. "Lock him up, Sergeant." He turned to Glenys. "We'll contact you later in the day, Miss Christopher."

She rose, and looked down at him. "Through Mr. Self. I won't be available any other way. May I ask why you are holding Mr. Callahan?"

"You may and you have," Trask said. "Good night, Miss Christopher."

Tommy said, "I'll be back, Brock. Get some sleep, kid. And don't go sounding off to any newspapers. I know quite a number of police officers. And every one of them earns every dollars he gets."

Pascal said, "This way, Callahan."

"Hold it a few minutes, Sergeant," Trask said.

Glenys patted my shoulder as she went by. Self smiled and nodded. They went out. Pascal closed the door and came back to stand next to the desk. His bloodhound's face was taut, weary.

Trask said, "Who the hell does she think she is?"

"A friend of the Governor's," I said.

"The Governor, that simple—"

"Easy, Dave," I interrupted. "Watch your tongue. You never know when Pascal may want to knife you for your job."

Pascal muttered something, and Trask's voice was edged. "You certainly have gone through a change of character, Brock. You're getting pretty big, aren't you?"

"No. I just don't like discourteous police officers. Most taxpayers don't, but most taxpayers don't weigh two hundred and seven pounds. Now, show me my bed; I'm sick and tired."

"You can sleep at home," Trask said. "I had to sound off at somebody, and you were available, Brock."

"All right, Dave. And Miss Christopher invulnerable. I know what you mean; she affects me the same way. But now that we're both too tired to fight, tell me one thing— do you honestly believe I would shield a murder, *at any level?*"

"I guess not, Brock. I'm too tired to argue. How did you get here? Is your car—oh, of course it wouldn't be. Sergeant, would you—"

Pascal's bloodhound face looked longer than ever.

Trask shook his head wearily. "No, you're right. You've been up as long as I have. Get any one of the boys who is around, or have a nearby car called in." He stood up. "That punk will break tomorrow, Sergeant. Report in late; get your sleep."

Pascal went out and Dave went to the water cooler. He

drank three paper cups full of water in succession and belched.

He came back to his desk and said, "I hope you're clean, Brock. It would be awfully damned bad for you if you weren't. Wait in the hall for your transportation. Close the door behind you."

He was dialing the phone as I went out.

A couple of traffic officers took me home. They weren't interested in me; they were baseball fans. They were moaning about the damned Yanks.

I didn't dwell on my lies or those of Glenys. I was too tired for conscience pangs; I was asleep two minutes after I'd pulled off my clothes.

In the morning, I managed to shower without getting my face wet. I made some coffee and picked up the *Times* outside my door.

There was a shot of me sleeping in Apoyan's office and a picture of Red Nystrom with his hands in front of his face. In the story under the pictures, there was a hint of "developments still to be disclosed, involving a prominent Southland family." This was a Wendell Lange quote, though he hadn't made the picture section.

It was now eleven o'clock and I wondered if the police had made any headway with Red or his young ally. I phoned Glenys Christopher.

"You poor thing," she said. "I've been sick all night, thinking of your face."

"Don't think about it. It's going to be fine. I was proud of you, but there will be records impounded, I can assure you."

"In time. Tommy tells me he can stall that indefinitely, almost. He's—young to be such a prominent attorney, isn't he?"

"He was always bright," I said. "Stanford man. You don't seem frightened today."

"I'm less frightened than I was, but I'm still frightened. I see Mr. Lange is quoted in the morning paper."

"That quote was for us, alone. If he really meant to blab, he could have. He wants to scare us but he doesn't want to alienate me. He's on the horns of a dilemma."

"That could have been fixed with a few dollars."

"And a piece of your soul. Damn it, girl, why should you knuckle under to thieves?"

"That's not quite it. We pay for our sins—and for our mistakes, Brock. I'd rather pay in money, because that's the easiest way."

"You didn't make the mistake," I pointed out.

"Yes, I did. I didn't watch his friends closely enough. I let him have his own way too much."

"All right, Aunt Glenys," I said. "I'll keep in touch with you."

"And be careful, please," she said.

"Yes'm," I said, and hung up.

By the time I got to the office, I was hungry, so I went over to the drugstore.

My fan behind the counter looked at me and shook his head sadly. "I read about it in the paper. You must be out of shape, Brock."

"Even at my peak," I told him, "I was vulnerable to .45's. How about one of those cheese and egg omelettes with some rye rolls?"

"Sure thing. Coming up." He went over the griddle to order it, and came back. "The boys are playing Fort Ord tonight, huh?"

I nodded.

"I hope they can stop that Matson."

I nodded, again. "How about a cup of coffee while I'm waiting?"

"Sure thing," he said. "Coming up."

Two people dead and one missing, but he worried about the Rams and the ponies. His world alive with wolves and tigers, but the big threat was the Forty-niners. He was only one of millions, and I'd been one of them myself until a few days ago.

Pretty country, jammed with geraniums. They take the place of lawns and are used to keep hills from eroding. They need very little water and come in a multitude of colors and can be planted from slips, and they spread like weeds. You'll hear strange rustlings in them, once in a while, but do not be alarmed. Rats live under the geraniums; they love the cover it provides them. The geranium jungle.

"Your coffee's cooling," my fan said. "You dozing, Brock?"

"I've been worrying about Ollie Matson," I said. "Do you think the boys can stop him?"

"Oh, well, it's only an exhibition game. Wait'll the season starts, and those Forty-niners come down to the Coliseum." He went over to get my omelette.

Outside, the prenoon traffic was quiet. A mixer whirred and my face itched and my mind went back over all of them. Bobby had been a hunch, based on the muscle-building equipment and Glenys' concern for a man she had forgotten too soon. I tried to find the ingredients for another hunch.

Somebody took the stool next to mine and said, "You damned fool."

I turned to see Jan Bonnet glaring at me. I smiled. "I didn't know you ate here."

"I don't. I went over to your office and you weren't

there. I saw your car in the parking lot and the attendant told me you eat here quite often." Her gaze seemed fascinated by the bandages. *"Why*—Brock?"

"It's cheap, and the food's fair."

"That isn't what I meant, and you know it. Why do you get carved up like a Thanksgiving turkey for a woman like Glenys Christopher?"

"Simmer down, honey. Have some lunch; it's almost noon."

"I want to know why."

"Honey, there are hockey players who take this in every third game they play. I'm being well paid."

"Don't call me 'honey.' You're not a honey-calling type."

"You should try the rye rolls here. They're great. And while you're eating, you could tell me why you stuck your neck so far out for Bobby. Because you know it's Bobby I worry about, not Glenys."

"I'm not worrying about either one of them, any more. I've washed my hands of the Christophers."

"All right. Now you can worry about me. I love it. But eat, build up your strength; I can be a problem for a real worrier."

"Don't sneer at me, Mr. Callahan."

"Believe me," I told her earnestly, "I'm not. I've been sitting here thinking about the lack of compassion in this world. It's—monstrous."

"You're serious, Brock?"

"I'm deadly serious. And I'm a little sick. And you're so damned comforting to be around. Have lunch with me, please."

"All right. Brock, it *is* Bobby, not Glenys?"

"It's Bobby," I said, "though I've no beef with Glenys."

"Of course not. We mustn't have any beef with the rich, must we? It's their world."

"Easy," I told her, "or you'll have a Congressional Committee on your neck. Let us not make subversive remarks about the well-to-do and especially not in Beverly Hills."

The counter man said, "To hell with the rich, if you ask me. I see 'em every day, and they don't look like much to me."

I wondered what he looked like to them. But I didn't voice it. Jan ordered a bacon and tomato sandwich and we ate in comparative silence.

Then, when I left her in front of the drugstore, she looked up and said quietly, "You wouldn't protect *anybody*, if you knew he was a murderer, would you?"

"I wouldn't. Neither a 'he' nor a 'she.' You don't think Bobby's a murderer, do you?"

"I don't. But wealthy people can fool you. They always look so clean and civilized and urbane. But we're all human."

"I know," I said. "Chin up, Jan."

She blew me a kiss and walked north. I watched her until she turned the corner.

In front of my office, I saw Juan Mira's car, but Juan wasn't in sight. When I came to the top of the steps, I saw him waiting in front of my office door. He had a *Times* folded under his arm.

His mahogany face was impassive, this morning. "I read the paper. Who is the rich family? They know about my Rosa?"

I unlocked the door without answering. I said, "Come in, Juan. Nobody seems to know about your Rosa."

"Who is the family?" he repeated. He stood just inside the doorway, glaring at me.

"It doesn't matter. Why do you want to know, Juan?"

"It matters. You tell me. I paid you. They paid you

more? They know about Rosa and paid you more?" He took out his wallet.

"Put it away, Juan," I said patiently. "I'm still looking for Rosa, but it's all blind alleys."

"You tell me the family. I find her. Rich people don't scare Juan. Beverly Hills people they are?"

"Good people, Juan. Fine, honest people. Don't make any trouble for them. I give you my word nobody has bought me."

"Then tell me the name."

I shook my head.

Scorn on his face, hate. "They bought you. But this Lange, he knows? I deal with him. I make you very damned sorry you double-crossed Juan Mira."

I went over to sit behind my desk. "Calm down, Juan," I said wearily. "I know as much as anybody you've read about in the papers, and I don't know where Rosa is. I'm still looking."

"You can stop," he said. "I find her. I find these rich people and they tell me. To hell with you, Brock Callahan."

He slammed the door behind him.

I looked up Lange's number and phoned him. His girl said he was due any minute. I gave her my number.

I was typing wearily away at the reports when he phoned. I told him, "There's a man named Juan Mira coming to see you."

"He's here now," Lange said. "He was waiting when I came back from lunch."

"Well, don't tell him anything. He's a fireball. He'll wind up in trouble and drag us along."

"Not me," Lange said. "You do go out of your way to protect the wealthy, don't you, Mr. Callahan? Mr. Mira has offered me one thousand dollars, just for a name."

"I wouldn't sell if I were you, Lange. Isn't there something in the California law about kidnaping applying to any person who is moved by force, even a few feet?"

"That's roughly it. Why do you ask?"

"Because Red Nystrom forced me to move a couple hundred feet last night, from my garage to my apartment."

"You weren't going to your apartment?"

"No, I wasn't. I was going to walk over to Wilshire and have something to eat, first. Red forced me to move against my will."

"I think Red has a different story on that. I think Red's story is that you asked him to come to your apartment because you wanted to bribe him not to reveal a young man's name. He laughed at you, and you attacked him."

"You know that's ridiculous," I said.

"I wonder if the police will? Red isn't too well loved by our Department friends, but then, neither are you, are you?"

"Lange," I said steadily, "if you give that little fireball the name he wants, I promise you you'll be sorry."

He chuckled. "Stop it, Mr. Callahan. You should know by now that I don't frighten that easily. Unless I get a better offer from a party of opposing interest, I will sell to any buyer. I don't live on hope—or threats. Good day, sir."

He hung up and I dialed the Christopher home. I told Glenys what had happened. I said, "Get Bobby out of town. Both of you get out of town. This Mira's a real hothead."

"Why can't we just pay Mr. Lange?" she asked. "How much did you say Mira offered him?"

"If you start paying Lange, you'll never stop," I told her. "If you don't want to leave town, phone the Beverly Hills police. They'll give you all the protection you need."

A pause, and then she said quietly, "All right, Brock. I'll do that. I'll phone the Beverly Hills police."

I went back to the reports and finished them. I drank two glasses of cold water and went over to the window to watch the traffic. I saw the Austin-Healey park across the street, and I saw Bobby get out and come my way. He, like Juan, had a paper with him.

He'd never looked more serious; I wondered if he was bringing bad news. I went to the door to meet him.

I asked him, "Did Glenys call the police for protection?"

He shook his head. "She phoned Lange." He opened the paper. "This is what I wanted to show you." He pointed to the picture of Pete Gonzales, the knife-wielding kid.

"Do you know him?" I asked.

"Only by name, and this picture. Rosa had a picture of him. He was her half-brother. He and Rosa had the same mother. She died about a year ago. Do the police know that?"

"I doubt it very much, Bobby. But I'll certainly tell them. Glenys phoned Lange, did she? What did she offer him?"

"I don't know, Brock. She's scared, and I can't argue with her. I tried to talk her out of it, but she said I'm the last person in the world she'd come to for advice."

I said, "Get in touch with Tommy Self, Bobby. Tell him what Glenys did. And now get out of here. If he can't get any satisfaction out of Lange, Mira will be back here. I don't want him to find you here."

"Okay, Brock. Will the police want me to testify about what I've told you?"

"Let's hope not. I'm going over there, right now."

Bobby went out and I locked the door and went down to my car. Bobby was out of sight, and I was pulling out of the parking lot when I saw Mira's Merc pull up in front of my office. I didn't stop and he didn't see me.

CHAPTER FIFTEEN

TRASK had just come in when I got to the West Side Station. He was talking to Caroline in his office. He didn't look happy to see me.

"Nystrom and Gonzales here?" I asked.

He shook his head. "Just the kid. We've transferred Nystrom downtown. Why?"

"Did the kid break, yet?"

Trask shook his head again. "What's on your mind, Brock? Learn something new?"

"The kid is Rosa Carmona's half brother. Did you know that?"

Trask paused, and shook his head for the third time. "Are you sure of it?"

I nodded. "Why don't I talk to him? Maybe he'd tell me more than he would a police officer. Haven't you got a room where we could be—overheard?"

Caroline looked more skeptical than Dave Trask, though Dave looked skeptical enough.

"What can you lose?" I asked him. "How much luck have you had, so far?"

Caroline muttered something. Trask said, "All right, Brock. I'll go along with it." He turned to Caroline. "Get a man on that room, try and get Ledsoe."

A little later, I went down the corridor with Dave Trask and a turnkey. In front of the kid's cell, Trask said loudly, "Don't ever go over my head again, Callahan, or you'll regret it. I'll give you ten minutes with this punk, for all the good that'll do you."

"Not in the cell," I answered. "I want to talk to him

177

privately. I don't want any of your stooges listening in The Captain said I could talk to him privately."

"He didn't tell me that," Dave said. "You want to wait until he comes back from lunch, and we can confirm it?"

The turnkey said, "Callahan's right, Lieutenant. Those were the Captain's orders."

We weren't exactly the Abbey Players, but pretty good for amateurs. The kid's inherently skeptical face showed no change, however.

Trask swore, and said, "All right. Ten minutes. They can use Room 23, officer." He went away, and a uniformed man came down the corridor.

The turnkey opened the cell door, and the uniformed man escorted us to a small room a few doors from Apoyan's office. The uniformed man stayed outside, and we could hear him locking the door.

It was a plain room with barred windows, holding some files and a cot and two chairs and a washbasin. I couldn't see any place where a mike would be concealed.

The kid went over to sit on the cot. "What do you want with me, footballer?"

"The same thing I wanted from Sue Ellen. Only Red stopped me from learning it. The only thing I've ever wanted in this whole mess. I want to know where Rosa Carmona is."

"How should I know?"

"Why shouldn't you? She's your half-sister, isn't she?"

Expression in the face now. Shock, and a tinge of fear. "Who told you that. Do the police know that?"

I shook my head. "Lange told me that. And he got it from Red. They're getting ready to sell you down the river, boy. They're saving it for the trial. But to hell with that; I'm here to find Rosa. And if you know, you'll tell

me where she is. She's got a mighty bright future if I
find her."

"You're lying. You're working for Mira."

I smiled. "Son, Mira has a few dollars, but not enough
to pay my kind of fees. Those Beverly Hills offices come
high."

"You mean—You're working—I mean, the guy *still*
wants to marry her?"

"Does that seem so strange to you? Rosa's a very attractive girl. She just seems to carry sunshine around with
her. Tell me, where is she?"

"I don't know," he said. "So help me, I don't know.
That rotten Scott was going to ruin her chances. He set
that up, didn't he, so she'd be found like that? Cut her off
from all that money, the son-of-a-bitch. And why? For the
guy's family, huh? They set it up, didn't they?"

"It doesn't matter. He's got his own money, now. He
came into it a week ago. And he wants to find her. How
come you went to the motel that night?"

"Red told me they were going to pull something on her.
When I got there, Scott was on the floor and Rosa wasn't
in sight. And I remember seeing this car pull away and I
realized the guy had been there and caught them."

"You didn't have to knife him, Pete. That solved nothing."

"Maybe I didn't knife him."

"All right, to hell with that. Where could Rosa have
gone; that's what we want to know now? Red killed her
friend, of course, but why should he do away with Rosa?
Maybe he only got her out of town. Maybe he didn't kill
her. What do you think?"

"Of course he didn't. Why should he?"

"Who knows why? Why should he kill Sue Ellen? He's

trying to plant that on you, too, but I'm damned sure it wasn't you running down the alley that night."

"Don't give me that, footballer. Red wouldn't rat."

"Wouldn't he? Who set you up to kill Scott? Why did he have to tell you about Scott's little trick?"

"Because he's a buddie, that's why. He's the boss."

"Cut it out. You're not *that* young. He wanted to get rid of Scott, so he could get some of those blackmailing pictures of Scott. He wanted that racket, but he was too stupid to realize it was no good without Scott's finesse. All he could milk was the old ones. He's got a beautiful way to set you up as the stooge, and when the time comes, he'll sing like a canary."

The kid took a deep breath and looked down at his hands. "I never trusted that Lange. He's a shyster, isn't he? He's no lawyer."

"In his business," I said, "he rides with the big boys in each case. In this case, Red's the big boy, and if he has to throw some minnows to the sharks to get Red off the hook, he'll do it. You're one of the minnows."

The kid was still looking at his hands. He said nothing.

I said, "There wasn't a reason in the world why Red should kill Sue Ellen, and you know it. She was Rosa's best friend, and she'd never rat. Red's kill crazy, or else he was afraid Sue Ellen knew what he had done to Rosa."

The kid was breathing heavily. He didn't speak.

"Unluckily for him," I went on, "I saw him running down that alley. That's one of those things nobody can figure in advance. That really put him in the soup. And when Red's cornered, he's out to protect Red—and no one else. You know that damned well, kid, and you're a sucker to let him pull it."

The kid looked up at me and his face was suddenly young. "Who have I got but Red and his shyster?"

"I'll get you some money; don't worry about that. You know my client's name?"

He shook his head. "I just know he's loaded."

"You know he didn't kill Scott."

He paused, and nodded. "I know that."

"And he didn't kill Sue Ellen."

The kid's pause was longer, this time. "Yes, I know that."

"All right, then, why should he be dragged into it?"

"I didn't know he was."

"Lange's trying to blackmail him. And where did Lange get his name, if you don't know it?"

"From Red?"

"Where else? And Red got it from Scott. And had you take care of Scott. Pete, think of how sweet they set you up. You're dead, right now, Pete."

He shook his head stubbornly. "No gas chamber for me. I'm too young."

"So you'll get life and ninety-nine years when Red and Lange get through crossing you. What you need is a good lawyer, with some money behind him, a lawyer who can point out to a female jury that you were in a rage, in temporary insanity, when you killed the man who despoiled your sister. You need a manicured lawyer for that, with some education behind him, not a cheap shyster who prejudices a jury against him the minute he opens his mouth."

"Footballer, you're not conning me?"

"You've got a right to think I could be, but just think back on everything I've told you. And if you know where Rosa is, now is the time to level. Believe me, I mean her no harm."

"I don't know where she is. That's the gospel. Look, could you get me some money for my defense? I'm not going to talk about anybody who'd spoil Rosa's chances."

"I'll get you some money. You give it to the police, exactly as you know it. You don't have to lie about my client. Give it all to them. Believe me, it's your best hope."

"I'll do it," he said. "And I'll give 'em the word on Lange, too. He's not as covered as he thinks he is. He was with Red a couple times when the law was looking for Red. I'll give 'em the word, all right."

I stood up. "Okay. And for the last time—you don't have any idea where Rosa could be?"

"I swear it."

I went over and knocked on the door, and the officer opened it. I said, "We're through," and looked at Pete Gonzales.

Pete said, "I want to make a statement. I want to confess." He took a breath. "And could you get the priest back? I'll talk to him now. It's Father Doyle, from St. Jude's."

In Trask's office, Trask was smiling. It wasn't a nice smile. "Good work, Brock. You're learning, aren't you?"

I shrugged. "I guess. I need a shower."

Trask continued to smile. "And the high and mighty Miss Glenys Christopher has a brother, hasn't she? Going to S.C., isn't he? I'm a UCLA man, myself."

"Don't make a disease out of it," I said. "You wouldn't throw the kid to the wolves, Dave. A man would need to be some son-of-a-bitch to do that."

"I've been called worse," he said.

"Not by me."

"Not yet. Where's this Rosa, that's what I want to know? Would young Christopher know that?"

"No."

"Would you?"

"You know I'm still looking for her. And your interest

in her comes a little late. You shrugged her off every time I mentioned her, before today."

He stretched and yawned. "Well, you go out and look for her. You find her, and maybe we can forget Bobby Christopher. Though that girl's scorn still rankles in my small soul."

I stood up and went over to the desk to use his phone. I got the Christopher residence, and Bobby answered.

I asked, "What's new on that end?"

"Tommy Self is here. We've got the money, five thousand in cash. Lange's dropping over to pick it up."

"Tommy okayed that?"

"He set it up. We have the serial numbers of the bills and a couple boys from the Beverly Hills Police Department ready to pick Lange up the minute he leaves with the money."

"That could put you in the soup, Bobby," I told him. "That could get you some headlines, when Lange starts to blab."

"Maybe not," he said. "Maybe not in Beverly Hills. We take care of our own up here, Brock. That's what Tommy thinks, anyway."

"Maybe," I said. "But if it gets out, be careful. There's a little hothead still looking for the name, you know."

"I'll be careful," he promised. "From here in, I'm the carefullest kid in the world."

Trask watched me replace the phone. "Now, what?" I told him.

His smile came back. "And those boys think they can sit on it? Wouldn't they be embarrassed if they knew I knew?"

"Wouldn't they, though? And wouldn't it be inconvenient for you, driving *around* Beverly Hills every time you wanted to go downtown?"

"Stop it," he said.

"I will if you will. If you have some charges against Bobby Christopher, go and get him. And you'll probably look even sillier proving them than you've looked up to now. Though that would be hard, I'll admit."

He stared at me without emotion. "We're off again, eh?"

"You're too hard to get along with, Dave. I've worked with you and for you and done my share. All I get are threats and your petty malevolence against the brother of a girl who wasn't impressed by you. You're too light to scare me and too petty to interest me. I hope I never have to work with you again."

Caroline came in with a sheaf of papers. "Sweet and complete," he said, "including his admission he drove the car that carried Red to and from the Venice murder of that Sue Ellen."

"Thanks to Brock Callahan," I said. "And on that grateful note, I'll leave. I've still got to find Rosa."

I was a step from the doorway when Dave said, "Just a second, Brock."

I stopped and turned.

Trask said, "Don't we shake hands? I want to thank you, Brock."

I went back to shake his hand.

And Caroline said, "Me, too. You're not a bad guy for a private peeper, Callahan."

"That's the way I feel about it," I agreed. "If anything rough comes up, feel free to call me in as a consultant."

A lot had happened since I'd had lunch with Jan. Too much had happened. I thought back to the lunch and our talk about rich people.

That was the thought that triggered my second hunch and the pieces fit. I swung the flivver toward Santa Monica.

It was one of the old, small Spanish houses with thick walls and small windows in a section of Santa Monica that was solid but not impressive. There were no new houses on the block, but the old ones were well kept up and the lawns were green. Clean, trimmed palm trees ran in symmetrical rows along both sides of the street.

I went along the walk to the front door, picking up the evening paper from the lawn on the way. There was no answer to my ring, though I could hear the heavy chimes inside.

I went out to the front again to see if there was any way to get to the back yard from here, but there was none, no gate in the high, concrete block wall that went back from the front of the house.

Coming back across the lawn I saw the partially open window. I paused and looked over at the house across the street. Nobody in sight. Nobody was looking my way on this side of the street. Well, Trask was my friend, now. Trask would take care of me.

I was halfway through the window when I realized Trask couldn't do me any good in Santa Monica, and this was Santa Monica. I almost went back out, but only almost.

The living room was high and beamed, a step down from the dining room. I went through it to the dining room, and through that to the kitchen. From here, I could look out into a walled rear yard, the walls covered with bougain-villaea, the yard bordered with geraniums. And what were those in the middle, on that arched trellis? Yellow roses, big as small cabbages.

I went back to the hall and into the largest bedroom. A picture of Rosa stared at me from the dresser. I opened the closet door and smelled a woman's fragrance. There was a woman's dressing gown hanging in here, and a couple dresses. There were some woman's shoes on the floor. There was a portable typewriter.

In the dresser, there were mostly men's clothes. There were only a few items of lingerie, and some stockings. I went over that room carefully and the other, smaller bedroom, but found nothing else of importance. Except for a loaded .32.

I went out into the backyard and over to the trellis. The lawn was mounded almost imperceptibly under the trellis and the sod looked like it had been recently replaced. I couldn't be sure; it was an excellent job of landscaping.

I went over to the geranium beds and it seemed to me the ground was higher than it should be, here, as though surplus ground had been added recently. I found some clumps of clay at the foot of the bougainvillaea. I went back to the trellis. Yellow roses for the faintly yellow Rosa; she did have some Chinese in her. Roses for Rosa? Who knew?

I went back into the kitchen and had some water and looked into the refrigerator for some beer, but there was none. There was some Coke, and there was some rum in the cupboard. I'd earned a drink of something hard; I mixed it and went back to the living room, to sit near the fireplace.

It wasn't more than ten minutes later that I heard a car stop in front, and I looked out the window to watch him get out and come up the walk.

I went over to open the door for him.

He was about six feet away when I opened the door, and he stopped short and glared at me. "How you get in? Why are you here?"

"I'm looking for Rosa, Juan," I said. "That's why you hired me, wasn't it?"

"How you get in? You are alone?"

"I'm alone. Come in, Juan."

He hesitated and then came the rest of the way to the door. He came in, and I left the door slightly ajar as I followed him into the living room.

He looked around in there, and then said, "You wait here."

"No. Not if you're going to get a weapon, Juan."

He shook his head. "No weapon. No cops, either. I look, first."

I went back to the fireside chair while he prowled the house. When he came back, he asked once more, "Why are you here?"

"I came to look for Rosa, but I realize now that wasn't why you hired me, was it, Juan?"

"You tell me, double-crosser. Why I hire you?"

"To find out all I could about Rosa and her friends. To find out who this last man she went with was, this *rich* man who wanted to marry her. The others didn't want to marry her, did they, Juan? They weren't going to take her away from you *permanently* like the rich man was."

Juan's hand was in his jacket pocket. Juan's face showed nothing but a hundred fights. "Big talk. What you prove?"

"Wealth bothered you too much," I explained. "You got indignant because I didn't think you were rich that very first day. When I told you about Red Nystrom, you asked if he was rich. So you knew it was a rich man Rosa liked."

He shook his head, staring at me.

"Today," I went on, "you talked about a Beverly Hills man. How did you know about a Beverly Hills man, Juan? Why do you hate the Beverly Hills men so much?"

"You tell me. Why?"

"You know why. Another thing, Juan—when that ring was returned, it was sent to your name *in care of me*. How many people knew I was working for you at that time?"

"Sue Ellen knew."

"Yes and Rosa would have known if she was alive. And *you* knew, Juan. That's three. It didn't seem sensible to me that either Sue Ellen or Rosa would give up a ring that valuable. There's nothing in their backgrounds that would make a gesture like that possible. So it had to be you, sending it to you. Which meant you had Rosa. And the postmark was Santa Monica; you're the only one of the three who lived in Santa Monica."

"And why would Juan kill Rosa?"

"Because she came to you, that night. When she ran from the motel, there was only one strong friend in the world she could trust. Out of desperation, she came here."

"You can't prove."

"I think I can. She came to you and you promised to protect her." I took a breath. "You told her now you would be married. And she turned you down, because she had a rich man who wanted to marry her, a young handsome, rich man from Beverly Hills. She probably laughed at you, didn't she, Juan?"

"Rosa never laugh at me. You know this man?"

"No, not for sure," I lied. "Do you know him, Juan?"

"I find out. Some cops know. I buy a cheap cop."

"Isn't one murder enough, Juan?"

"Without Rosa, who cares? But the man who took my Rosa, I get him. I get that bastard first. Then the cops can have Juan."

I shook my head. "No, Juan. I work with the law."

"Like hell," he said. "For the rich, you work. Against the law, you work."

I shook my head. "You only came to me because of the Beverly Hills address. You thought I might know about the man because of that."

"No. I trust you. I see you at the Coliseum, many times.

You are my favorite Ram. But you cheat me, you do not give me what I pay for."

"You paid me to find Rosa, Juan," I reminded him. "And I think I've found her. Is it Rosa, under that rose trellis?"

He stared at me and the hand came out of the jacket pocket and the .32 was in it. "Bastard Brock Callahan," he said. "The yard is big enough for you, too."

"Put it away, Juan," I said. "It's empty. I've got the shells in my pocket."

Sergeant McCall was a fat man and flustered. I said, "Get Lieutenant Dave Trask over at the West Side Station. He'll be interested. This all ties in with that Roger Scott killing in Brentwood."

"We don't need any L.A. police officers in Santa Monica," he said irritably. "We can handle our own affairs." He looked out the kitchen window, to where some men were digging. "Man. you'd better be right about this, or it'll be your neck."

"I'm not doing the digging," I said. "And I haven't the authority to order you to dig. You should have faked some kind of gas leak report, or something."

"All the utilities come in from the front, peeper."

"Callahan's the name," I said. "Brock Callahan. All-League for five years, you may remember."

"Wise son-of-a-bitch, aren't you?" he said. "My God, they've struck something out there." He went out the kitchen door.

I picked up the phone quickly and got the West Side Station. Trask wasn't there, but Pascal was. I told him the story quickly, and said, "Don't tell anybody I phoned. This sergeant over here hates my guts."

"I can understand that," Pascal said. "Okay, we'll call the Chief." He hung up without thanking me.

One of the diggers was sucking at his hand, where a rose thorn had scratched it. The other one was bending over the hole, taking dirt out by the handfuls, now, working carefully. Sergeant McCall bent over as far as his obesity would permit. Then he went to his knees, and started taking out some dirt, himself.

I mixed another rum and coke and went into the living room. In the Department car in front, I could see Juan Mira sitting between two uniformed men. They didn't even want to take him down until they had something. Santa Monica takes care of its own, like Beverly Hills.

Juan had caught me once, under the heart, and the little man could still hit. I had a bruise under the heart. But a good little man is not a match for even an ordinary big man if the big man is careful.

Sirens, and an ambulance came up across the street, looking for a driveway to turn in. I went into the bedroom for my last look at Rosa's picture. I didn't want to see her when they pulled her out of the hole. I'd never seen her, and I sure as hell didn't want this to be my first look.

I heard steps in the kitchen, and went out. One of the diggers was getting a glass of water from the sink. He gulped as I looked at him anxiously.

"Well—?" I finally asked.

"A girl all right," he said. "Wrapped in silk, no less. That digging is sure hot work." He looked at the rum and coke. "You cheap peeper, drinking a citizen's booze."

I got home a little after eight, and I had my shower. I was going to put on a robe and relax, but I decided against that. I didn't want to be alone with myself, not after today's work. I wasn't real proud of myself, though it had been a full day's work.

I put on a lightweight suit and a cotton sport shirt and went out into a fairly warm evening. I climbed into the flivver and drove north, toward Sunset. I had half a mind to go over to Christopher's, though I wasn't really looking forward to it. I'd had enough of the Christophers today.

On Beverly Glen, the flivver seemed to turn itself, and go scooting up toward the hills. I swung it off to the left at the narrow side road and looked ahead anxiously to see if there was a light.

There was a light.

No sound from the dog as I went up the stepping stones. My heart hammering a little as I rang the bell.

Jan came to the door and looked up puzzledly. "Nothing wrong, I hope?"

"Everything all straightened out, except for a few ends. Are you—expecting company?"

"Not exactly, though I was hoping someone would drop around. I don't feel like going out, though."

"Neither do I," I said. "Look, Jan, this—I mean, I'm probably bad company. But you talked about a—a need. And I certainly need someone tonight. It's been a miserable day, and I'm a little sick of myself."

"It hasn't been the best day in the world for me, either," she said, and smiled up at me. "But it's getting better. Won't you come in, Doctor Callahan?"

END